TWO ONCE SETTLED

Two Once Removed Series Book 3

Milo Hays

www.milohays.com

INTRODUCTION

Two Once Settled is the third of three books in the Two Once Removed series. Readers should have read both Two Once Removed and Two Once There to get full enjoyment of this story.

1

The thick, oversized, off-white linen envelope stood out in the pile of forwarded mail that sat on the coffee table. The elegant, hand-scribed address on the front, paired with the large, embossed *W* and typeset return address on the back flap, proclaimed it was special, long before the recipient had the opportunity to open it.

Jason Cartwright studied the envelope as he settled into the living room sofa that faced the cabin's view of the deck and budding treetops that surrounded it. Early April, springtime was erupting all around the property, and the staged arrival of blossoms and pollens was about to begin.

The Great Falls return address was familiar to him from his time living in Northern Virginia near Washington, DC thirty years earlier. It was the home community of his former fiancée, Callie Larson, whom he schemed to reconnect with sixteen months earlier in the event her marriage had collapsed, as his had. And, if so, to see if there was potential for the two of them to couple for their empty-nest years.

Addressed to his beach cottage, the obvious invitation was delivered almost two weeks later to Jason's mountain cabin community called Fox Farm. Fox Farm was a fifty-acre mountain farm that was restored to host twelve secluded cabins appointed with fine attributes and comfort. The target audience for Fox Farm was any person, couple, or family seeking to either tour the Asheville/Lake Lure area of North Carolina or looking to escape from the world. Jason discovered the property while visiting over Christmas when his four daughters spent the holidays with their mother.

Jason bought Fox Farm as it sat on the verge of bankruptcy, securing a lucrative and fun business venture along with the services of one of its founders, Clara Haigh. Years earlier, Clara and her husband, Tom, purchased and renovated the then-abandoned mountain property. Tom died from pancreatic cancer soon after Fox Farm opened for business. His medical bills, along with the property's lost business through his illness, had put their dream in jeopardy when Jason and his Chesapeake Bay Retriever, Zoe, arrived for their two-week stay on Christmas Eve.

Jason's Christmas and New Year's visit gave him the opportunity to see the operation and to talk to Clara about her business. As a serial entrepreneur throughout his career, Jason always wondered about how founder ideas evolved into working businesses.

Jason first talked with Clara on Christmas Eve when she hosted a small, informal Christmas celebration at the farm's main house. Their initial conversation was full of great expectations for the New Year that both were seeking. As they crossed paths through the week, their conversations became more comfortable, opening a candidness that led to his discovery of the property's challenges and Clara's need to sell.

Jason moved the rubber band–bound pile of mail to the middle of the coffee table to ensure that he would not forget about it. As he rested his athletic, six-foot-four-inch, fifty-seven-year-old body into the soft cushions of the living room couch, he took a pull of coffee to replace his lingering endorphin high with caffeine. His morning run, which was a poor replacement for his morning ocean swims, allowed him to start his days with a better frame of mind, as well as to keep unwanted pounds off. The comforting wind-down and boost he was feeling melded with the scenery that surrounded the Flying Dutchman cabin. He was happy to be in the mountains.

As Jason closed his eyes to recline deeper into the cushions, two hands grazed over his shoulders from behind then washed down his chest. Jason felt his body tense as he inhaled sharply and dropped the envelope. His hands immediately reached to take hold just as the arms clenched on him into a hug that was followed by a warm, soft kiss on his neck. He could feel the heat of her body transfer to the back of his neck as she tasted the residual salt from his sweat.

The lean she needed for her surprise embrace put her in jeopardy. It was enough for Jason to grab, pull, and pin her to the couch cushions behind him. A shriek of laughter erupted as she squirmed under his total control of her body. As he approached to kiss her, she abruptly squirmed and turned to bury her face and laughter into the cushions.

Her playful reaction to his countermove caused Jason to stop and wait out her eventual need for air. A smile came to his face as he watched a panic appear on hers as she searched for options. When she finally turned to see his face smiling, her eyes lit as she kissed him before he could make his move. She then collapsed back onto the cushions, waiting, smiling, for him to respond.

"Make love to me again," she proposed.

Jason ran his hand along the contours of her slim, forty-eight-year-old body to ponder the idea. The feel of her skin through his college t-shirt, followed by a light snap of the waistband of his flannel boxer shorts she was wearing, brought a smile to his face. As she felt his palm gently caress her inner leg, a smile appeared on his face.

"I am fifty-seven and just finished a three-mile cross-country run," he mumbled while continuing to play with her waistband. "Besides, that just may be too much of a good thing."

"Just GOOD!?"

"Did I say *GOOD?*... I meant.... AWESOME!" he clarified, then smiled.

"Well," Clara replied, as she shuffled out of his grasp and on to her feet, "if you have to think about it, and you think it's too much, OLD MAN, then you don't get it."

Jason moved to grab her hand to pull her back. Just missing, Clara started to step back as she smiled. She then playfully darted to the bedroom without looking back. Amused by her foreplay, Jason reclined back into the cushions to wait.

"Really?" she questioned, sticking her head out the door to find him still on the couch.

Getting what he wanted, Jason jumped to take a superman pose. As Clara laughed, the mysterious envelope fell to the floor and was kicked under the couch. Clara then screamed as he dashed toward her, to disappear with her into their bedroom.

# # #

Callie was seated in their usual corner of Starbucks as she watched the continuous roll of caffeine addicts flow in and out of the store. Many were her age. More were kids looking for their daily dose of caffeine.

The rain and unusually cold late April weather had created an ache in her trim, fifty-year-old body that she was hoping to shake. Her go-to mocha latte, made with skim milk and sweetened by two packets of sweet-n-low, was her favorite cold-weather remedy. The first taste soothed her taste buds as its warmth flowed down into her chest.

"Sorry I'm late," pulled her back into the moment.

Sandy Worth, Callie's best friend from childhood, dropped a canvas bag next to the table as she removed her wet windbreaker.

"This wedding is going to kill me."

Callie smiled at her friend's statement. Although a daunting endeavor, the challenge of a wedding for Sandy's twenty-five-year-old daughter seemed small in comparison to Callie's past year. A wedding is a joyful event with many fun details. It should be exciting to plan. And although Sandy was about to explode under the pressure of getting it all done well, she was also beaming with excitement that her oldest, and only daughter, was getting married.

"I haven't heard from a lot of people," Sandy added. "I don't know what's so hard about checking a box, writing your name, and mailing back an already addressed AND STAMPED envelope."

Callie's aches evaporated with the distraction that Sandy had brought to the table. The canvas bag at her feet held a leather portfolio packed with loose pieces of paper. Callie noticed some were simple notes in Sandy's cryptic handwriting. Others were printed contracts with print too small to read.

Callie turned her body to the table as Sandy began to unpack her papers. In addition to the leather portfolio that acted as her working desk, she also had a three-inch, expandable, accordion folder Callie remembered her dad used regularly in his work as a lawyer.

"Looking at this makes me glad that two out of my three kids are boys," Callie said as Sandy focused on organizing her papers. "Ja —"

Callie's words and Sandy's actions stopped on her stutter of Jason. It was the first time since July that Callie had mentioned Jason Cartwright in conversation. Callie could feel a twitch in her cheeks as pressure began to build in her eyes. His image appeared in front of her as it was on the day when Callie not only buried her mother but sent him away so she could resurrect her failed marriage.

Callie struggled to forget Jason, often entering his name in her Facebook search when her marriage with Chase seemed to be turning dark again. Entering his name was as far as she could take it. She knew looking at anything related to him would reignite wanting what could not happen. She would often close Facebook with his name still in the search bar instead of deleting it to move on.

"If his girls want anything like Maddie does," Sandy added just to move the conversation, "that news article on what he got for selling his company better be true.... And it still may not be enough."

Sandy smiled as she watched Callie stay motionless. Callie's lower cheek started to quiver as she continued to sit in thought. Jason Cartwright was her first love. Jason would say what she felt made him her ONE. The person who, above all others, was perfect for her. Jason admitted to Callie that she was his ONE when they reconnected near his beach house sixteen months earlier. A post he put on Facebook found its way to Callie to entice her to find him.

What Callie originally planned to be a quick down and back from her mother's house to sneak a look at him and his new life, changed when they accidentally crossed paths at a gas station near his small beach cottage.

"Yeah," Callie agreed. "He's going to spend a fortune. I'm sorry you didn't get to meet them at Mom's funeral. They're quite a neat blend of personalities."

"Well," Sandy said while rolling her eyes. "Jason promised to talk to me after the funeral then disappeared."

"Yeah, sorry." Callie winced, knowing that her decision to stay with her husband after deciding to divorce him was the reason.

"It's OK, he's—"

Sandy stopped her acceptance of the apology. Although he had not responded to the invitation, he was invited along with a plus-one. The histories of their families and shared childhoods in Cleveland, made not inviting either Jason or Callie impossible.

Jason's best friend growing up was Sandy's older brother Mark. He was flying in from England for the wedding and asked if Jason was on the invitation list. His turnaround time in DC was going to be short. Sandy expected that Mark would connect with Jason to bring him to DC over the wedding weekend anyway.

That reunion would pull him away from the wedding she was spending a fortune to give. The two needed to see each other. Their last connection was over five years earlier when Jason and his now ex-wife, Stephanie, were in London visiting their daughter Rachel who was finishing a semester abroad at Oxford University. The two men were inseparable as boys. Sandy felt a special obligation to invite Jason, despite his recent events with Callie.

"He's what?" Callie inquired.

Callie paused to watch Sandy struggle with her answer.

"Jesus Christ, Sandy," Callie stated. "You can't be serious?"

"I'm sorry," she replied, wincing.

"I guess we can't come then."

"You can come," Sandy replied. "I've taken care of things."

Sandy reached into her canvas bag to find a folded floor plan for the reception. Great Falls Country Club had a large ballroom capable of seating up to three hundred people for dinner while hosting a full band and dance floor. Sandy unfolded the table scheme, placing their coffee cups and a tabletop ad stand to hold the corners down.

"Look," she said. "I have you and Chase over here with the Beards and the Schmitts. That will be company for you to keep Chase occupied."

"They'll see each other," Callie stated. "I'll see him. And I don't think I can handle that."

"It'll be OK. He'll be sitting with Mark and Jen," Sandy pleaded. "Those two will be so engaged with each other that Jason won't even notice you."

Callie responded with a cold stare of disbelief. Jason Cartwright may not notice Chase in a crowd. But he would feel Callie, just as she would feel his presence too. Knowing he was near would also heighten her senses to him. Chase seeing Jason was also bound to create opportunities for him to create trouble. With alcohol, Chase would be unencumbered to say something rude and provocative. And Jason may just have his restraint dulled enough to make a run at him.

"Sandy, seriously," Callie pleaded.

"I had to... Mark asked. Our families..."

Callie felt her stomach pit as she thought through the likely responses she would get by either telling Chase that Jason would be at Maddie's wedding, or by acting dumb until Jason's arrival at the wedding itself. Neither had potential to work better than the other. Chase would likely declare that neither he nor Callie would attend the wedding, which would offend her best friend. Or, he would go, get a few drinks in him, then attack Jason either verbally or with fists flying. That, too, would offend Sandy and likely get them banished from the country club.

"Has he responded?" Callie asked, hoping a conflict could eliminate her problem.

"Not yet."

"When was it due?"

"Friday."

"He's never late," Callie mumbled, hoping something was amiss.

Sandy watched as her friend got lost in thought. She knew his presence at Maddie's wedding was going to be problematic for both of them. Sandy had been Callie's rock since July, when Callie both buried her mother and resurrected her dead marriage. The single event, which Callie read as the absolute dissolution of her family, caught Jason in the crosshairs to send him home without her.

"I'm really sorry," Sandy implored.

Callie smiled to accept the apology her best friend did not have to give. She knew Sandy was stuck through an obligation to her brother, and their families, to invite Jason. She also knew Jason would be there for the same reason. He would also expect to see her there with Chase. Sandy's eyes welled with sympathetic tears for her friend who had been struggling for so long.

"Well, if he shows, I'll get through it," Callie smiled. "And Maddie will have the best fucking wedding ever imagined."

Sandy smiled at Callie's renewed confidence and enthusiasm.

"Atta girl," she responded as she reached to comfort her best friend.

2

The thick, oversized, off-white linen envelope returned to sit upright on the coffee table. Its exterior had a few dents and wrinkles from being stepped on while resting under the couch next to its center leg. An imprint of Jason's work boot was embedded on its top left corner.

Clara noticed the envelope while completing some light housekeeping. Their time in the cabin was ending soon as paying customers were scheduled to arrive in two days. That reality meant that she and Jason had to move back to the smaller, main house living quarters.

Clara studied both sides of the envelope for its quality, thickness, and the hand-written calligraphy addressed to Mr. Jason Cartwright. The inscribed address was his beach house six hours away. The United States Postal Service added its own nicks and bruises along with a few postmarks, barcodes, and a forwarding sticker. The elegant invitation, to an obviously grand event near Great Falls, Virginia, was only for him. The only *W* Clara could think of had been out of office for several successive terms. She was eager to see if it included a plus-one.

"Oh my God!" Jason remarked as he saw the envelope.

"It was kicked under the couch."

"Among other things," he observed as he opened it.

Clara watched as Jason pulled the contents from the envelope. She noticed an interior envelope of the same paper. Jason's name was written in the same calligraphy. Inside the envelope was a card with a series of names and words similar to the old-world wedding invitations she and Tom considered during their engagement. The cost and time to create that level of invitation made them opt for a standard typeset invitation that she was happy to think about until seeing this one.

"Holy smokes," she remarked as Jason finished reading the invitation and sifted through the balance of the included items.

Jason grimaced as he looked at the response card, then at his watch.

"She's going to kill me," he said.

"Who? Why?"

"Sandy... Sandy Fisher, I mean, Sandy Worth," Jason clarified. "Sandy... Fisher... Worth."

Still focused on the invitation, Jason repeated Sandy's name in a slow cadence using a clenched chin, low-pitched, snobby voice.

"She's a childhood friend from Cleveland. Her daughter is getting married. Her older brother, Mark, was my best friend growing up. That's likely why I got invited."

"That's fun. And?" Clara posed, looking for the plus-one she wanted.

"It's late. I also promised her at Callie's mother's funer—" Jason paused. "Shit."

"What?"

"Callie will be there too. She's Sandy's best friend."

Clara's enthusiasm for the plus-one plummeted as she envisioned Jason seeing Callie again. Their split in July just about emotionally killed him. Although he admitted he deserved the payback from their original engagement that ended with substantial pain for her, their split in July was driven by different circumstances not related to either her or her feelings for him. It was the result of the convergence of her looming divorce, her mother's death, her losing control to the point of striking one of her sons for a rude comment to her, and her children's disappointment in their father, who cheated. That disappointment also rippled to Callie for allowing it to affect them.

Callie and Clara met at Fox Farm before she started dating, loving, then living with Jason. Callie's appeal and allure to Jason was obvious and undeniable. It was fortunate for Clara that Callie's mother's passing ended Callie's need to visit Williamsburg where her mother lived. Great Falls, Virginia was more than twice the distance to Jason's Outer Banks beach cottage. It was even farther from Fox Farm in the western North Carolina mountains. Clara felt secure that Callie was out of range for Jason until he mentioned her name as part of the wedding's guest list.

"Is there a plus-one?" Clara asked, joking to hide her determination to keep her claim on her man.

Jason looked again, then smiled.

"Yes," he answered, shifting his eyes from the smaller interior envelope to Clara's. "Want to go to DC?"

"I wouldn't miss this." Clara laughed nervously. "But if it's late, you should call her."

Jason nodded agreement as he pondered the presence of Callie, her husband, and her children at the ceremony and reception. The vision in his head excited and depressed him at the same time. He did not want to go.

"I'll call her to accept, and to apologize for being late. I'm sure Sandy will sit us across the room with Mark to separate us from Callie and that asshole husband of hers," Jason thought out loud.

His eyes glossed over again as his thoughts finished. Clara could see the projector playing in his head. He was envisioning something to do with Callie's husband that was not a good precursor to the upcoming event. Clara knew she had ten days to work the schedules for management coverage at Fox Farm to be able to go with him for the wedding weekend.

"You know, you'll have to behave yourself," she clarified, half joking and half afraid. "He'll likely have friends there."

"Let's hope so." Jason replied, returning to her with a refreshed gleam in his eye.

# # #

"Do you want the good news? Or the bad news?"

Callie stopped short of their regular Starbucks table as she heard the questions. Her goal today was to visit with her friend to ask for advice and support. Instead, Sandy blindsided her with questions that had answers she was not going to like.

"You tell me," Callie answered as she removed her black Patagonia wind jacket.

Sandy smiled at the humor of her upcoming clarification, only to lose her amusement as she realized that the news was going to hurt.

"The answer's the same either way," she said. "Jason's coming with a plus-one."

Callie closed her eyes to the news as she slumped heavily into the chair. A pressure started to mount in her chest as the thought of being near him. A vision of him and Chase near each other again appeared on her mental screen.

"Fuck," she mumbled. "I was afraid of that and hoping to avoid it when you said he didn't reply."

"I'm sorry," Sandy replied while watching her best friend struggle with the news. "He called. Said the mail forward, and something about under a couch, caused him to miss the deadline."

"And you couldn't just tell him, too bad, too sad?"

Sandy smiled at the question. She could see and feel Callie's struggle. She felt responsible, again, for the pain she was causing Callie that related to Jason.

The first time was when she reintroduced them almost thirty years ago to start the dating that led to their engagement, and to its cancellation five weeks before the wedding. The second time was showing her his Facebook post last fall as a tease. The third was going to be putting them in the same room at Maddie's wedding.

It was easy for anyone to see the connection that Jason and Callie had then and now. Callie's decision to cut Jason loose again in July had been weighing heavily on her. To put them in the same room again, now, was picking an old scab off a wound that was never going to heal.

"This is such a bad time for this," Callie whispered sadly. "That's why I wanted to meet you today."

"What's wrong?"

"Everything," she answered. "Jason was right. Chase is acting weird. It seems like he's pulling away again. I can feel it."

"I don't believe that. He's learned his lesson."

Callie laughed at Sandy's choice of words.

"Lesson," she responded, repeating the word that made her laugh. "Like it's that simple."

"I didn't mean to make light of it," Sandy answered.

Callie watched her friend squirm as she maneuvered to fix her word choice. Sandy was not getting any of it.

"Do you know what it's like to sleep with someone who's cheated on you?" Callie asked.

"I hope not," Sandy answered with a nervous laugh that started and ended quickly.

"All you see in his face is him with some other woman," she answered, ignoring Sandy's failed humor. "All I see in his face is him with some faceless girl. She's blonde and laughing. They're laughing. Likely at me."

Callie's eyes shut again as her body rocked side to side. Sandy studied her friend's new, depressed demeanor and worried about the confession she was hearing.

"Callie, I'm sure Chase is being faithful to you."

Callie's body lifted as it stiffened. Her face lit with a forced smile as her tearing eyes opened.

"What is wrong with me?" she asked. "Why is God crapping on me constantly with two men who both swept me off my feet, then just shit all over me?"

Callie waited as she watched Sandy process the questions she could not answer. A look of empathy appeared on Sandy's face, hoping to give comfort to her friend when words escaped her.

"Well, if the first one can make such a huge about-face, to make an even bigger effort to win you back, there's hope that number two will see the same light and do the same."

"I don't know," Callie mumbled. "Jason had twenty-seven years to make his change. Chase was given twenty-seven hours from the time my mom died to the time I agreed that we could try again."

Sandy remained quiet as Callie pondered her own words. Although both men pulled away from her, their circumstances and sins were very different. Their reasons for reconciliation were also very different. Jason did not choose to abandon her weeks before their wedding. She dropped him when she saw he could not either accept or handle the responsibility and commitment of being married. Chase chose, on many different occasions, to violate his wedding vows to have one-night-stands and ongoing relationships with a variety of women on the campaign trail.

Chase's last affair lasted over a year and was still happening in Nantucket when he personally delivered their children Lizzie and Will to see Callie's mom just before she died. He promised Callie to end it permanently if she agreed to take him back. Callie never fully trusted that he severed the ties of that affair. Her faith held her to believe that if he did not end it with that woman, God would provide a way to uncover his continued disloyalty along with a new path to happiness.

"You also have over twenty-five years with Chase, three glorious kids, and a rich, wonderful life," Sandy added to help rebuild Callie's hope and enthusiasm.

"Rich, yeah," she answered. "His income and my family's money. I'm not so sure which is more important, not him."

"That's something we all have to deal with," Sandy empathized. "My dad locked mine away in a trust."

"I wish I had your dad," Callie replied, then regretted the thought as it left her lips. "My dad insisted we combine everything, fully expecting my marriage to be lifelong like his."

Callie paused to think, then smiled.

"That was actually a fight Jason and I had. I had more than he had, and he didn't want me to do that. Said it was 'stupid.' I took it as a sign of non-commitment. He was just saying he wanted to marry me, for me."

Callie stared at the cup in front of her as she ran the thought back through her head. Realistically, she knew he was probably keenly aware of the potential for his inner demons to push them apart. His insistence that their money not commingle was his insurance for her, that she would always have her parent's legacy gift. But she also could not shake the thought that his explanation was honest. That money was not why he wanted to marry her. They were going to take on the world together. They did not need her, or his, *family money* to *make it*.

Sandy sat quietly as she watched Callie continue to process the events of the past and present. Her blank expression shifted to a smile as she exhaled lightly with a laugh.

"I'm such an idiot."

# # #

Google maps estimated that the drive from Fox Farm to the plush Willard Hotel in Washington, DC would take eight hours.

An earlier estimate was thirty minutes shorter. But that was processed at night, with an after-midnight arrival. Leaving in the morning would put their arrival in the middle of rush hour.

The morning air was cool and left a wet residue on the car. As Jason loaded their suitcases into the back of his Volvo Cross Country station wagon, Clara finished giving last-minute instructions to her number one, Ruth, who covered for her from time to time as she traveled with Tom, and later to chase and travel with Jason.

"Clara," he said. "We have to get going."

"OK," she said while turning from Ruth to cross the dew-covered grass to the car. "I don't know what the fuss is. We have more than enough time, and you declined the rehearsal dinner."

Jason smiled at Clara's slight whining to his push to get going. Her comment was right. But he still wanted to get moving so they would arrive early enough to enjoy a nice romantic dinner in the nation's capital. The recommended hotels near the reception were abundant, and far less expensive, than the room he reserved at the Willard. But this was an opportunity to live a little beyond the comforts of what Clara created in the mountains, and what he created at the beach. He also wanted to front-load the weekend with focus on her before exposing her to the unknowns of the wedding and his unavoidable reconnection with Callie and her husband.

As Jason shifted the Volvo into drive, he looked to Ruth to wave goodbye. Jason's Chesapeake Bay Retriever, Zoe, sat next to Ruth on the main house side porch, eagerly waiting for his call to join them. With Zoe focused on the car, Ruth slowly took hold of her collar. A hand wave of her free hand told Jason it was now good to start their trip.

Zoe tugged slightly before acquiescing to Ruth's hold. She whined as she watched the car drive off the property and down Blackburn Road. Once out of sight, Zoe looked to Ruth, then returned to the kitchen to find something to eat.

3

The late-April evening Northern Virginia air was cool and held a freshness that confirmed spring was in full bloom. Callie pulled her Range Rover around to the garage, disappointed to have missed an open-window drive home from the salon. She had a full work-up of haircut, set, then nails for the rehearsal dinner. As she pulled into the garage, she noticed Chase's Maserati was not parked in its bay. He was running late and did not either text or call her.

"I don't believe it." she mumbled, as his garage door light lit and the sound of a revving engine filled the air.

Callie waited as the blue Maserati he bought without telling her came to a stop next to her. When she looked, she saw him grab his phone, rev the engine one last time, then look at her with a devious smile. Her forced, exaggerated smile sent the message she no longer thought it was cute, and that he was late.

"I'm sorry," he said apologetically as he emerged from his car. "I got caught in traffic."

"It's OK," Callie replied as she brushed by him. "You'll be ready long before I am. Would you please pour me a *dresser* to get ready?"

Chase was happy to hear that Callie both recognized that his late arrival would not impact their departure time to the rehearsal dinner. He was also delighted to hear her request for a drink, a *dresser*, which was a warm-up to relax for the evening. Her asking for one implied that she would not criticize him for having one with her.

Chase arrived at the door to their master suite holding a bourbon on ice in his right hand and Callie's healthy pour of rosé in his left. His bourbon started as a double which he halved between the bar and their bedroom. A single pour for him would be acceptable even with her large pour of wine to get them started.

Callie emerged from the bathroom covered in a slip. Her eyes looked to him with the message to point her to her drink. His eyes glanced to the wine sitting on her nightstand near where her dress for the evening lay. As she watched him look to her nightstand with a nod, she checked the pour of his bourbon before turning to take a pull from her nerve calmer.

"Thank you," she said right as she lifted the glass to her lips. "This is very helpful."

Chase watched Callie take a drink. She then closed her eyes as the wine permeated her taste buds then found its way to her bloodstream. It had a visible calming effect on her as she rocked back and forth in thought.

"I've got something to tell you," Callie said as her eyes shifted from closed to look at him.

Chase stood in anticipation of some good news as his wife stood before him half dressed. He took a small taste of bourbon in anticipation.

"Jason will be probably be at dinner tonight, and the wedding tomorrow."

Chase choked on his bourbon as the news arrived. He quickly placed his hand to his mouth as he moved the glass away. He struggled to regain his composure while Callie enjoyed his struggle.

"Why?" Chase asked, then stopped to think. "Oh, Sandy... you... him... Cleveland."

"I just wanted you to know going in, and not be surprised."

Chase watched for Callie's expression to shift from serious to empathy. He was disappointed to see her remain serious as she watched his reaction to the news.

"That motherfucker is never going to get out of our lives," he mumbled. "Where are my brass knuckles?"

Although joking, Callie stood taller to ensure her message was clear. He was not to do anything to either incite or in any way aggravate any part of the evening or weekend.

"Park all of your animosity right here, right now," Callie demanded. "You will be cordial and social. And don't think drinking will excuse any bad behavior."

Callie's orders infuriated Chase. He would maintain decorum during any interaction with Jason Cartwright. But this was his turf. It was his country club. His friends would be around him, and they would come to his aid if anything erupted with Callie's first lover. He thought about the potential to take Jason outside to pummel him. Where. How. When. He started nodding his head as the vision grew clearer.

"I know that look," Callie said to bring him back. "Nothing, Chase. He'd kick your ass, anyway."

Chase exhaled as he smiled. The smug look on his face brought concern to Callie. The two men would have to be kept separate. But she did want to see Jason, talk to him, and touch him, one more time.

# # #

Jason noted his GPS estimated their arrival at The Willard would be at eight minutes after six in the evening. The estimate shifted up and down by as much as thirty minutes as he crossed North Carolina, stopped, and drove I-95 North up through Richmond toward Washington.

As they drove the Richmond beltway around the city, both Jason and Clara noticed the signs and two-lane exit that redirected traffic from the beltway onto Interstate 64 toward Williamsburg, and the Outer Banks. Jason felt a twinge in his stomach as they passed the exit, thinking about Callie nine months earlier at the cemetery. The vision was as clear as it was when he was there. He could see Callie's tear-streaked face while his subconscious took over driving his car.

"Are you OK?" Clara asked, noticing Jason had completely checked out at eighty miles per hour. "Jason!"

Jason jerked as he came back to real time. He repositioned in his seat as he reoriented his eyes and attention back onto the road. Once composed, he looked to Clara with a smile.

"Do you want me to drive?" she asked.

"No, I'm fine."

"You were hours down that road to the beach," she declared.

"I'm back now."

"Am I going to regret being your plus-one?"

"Absolutely not," he answered with a renewed smile and pat on her leg. "This will be a fun weekend."

Clara did not respond to his answer. Her face said she was still concerned about his tune-out.

"Seriously," he said. "I have a surprise for you."

Clara answered with a slight laugh and head shake. She closed her eyes to the thought of what was coming. She and Jason were six months into their romantic relationship. His return after the funeral and time alone at the beach started their coupling nicely with a passion-filled hug. Their romance advanced slowly as each was reluctant to leave the comfort of their isolation to discover the love they both knew could be perilous. Their relationship had been employer/employee before they became interested in each other.

Clara always felt divine intervention delivered Jason after Tom died and Fox Farm was close to foreclosure. She also believed that God acted again, with divine inspiration, to give her the courage to chase after him and declare her romantic interest in him before Callie's hold became too strong to break. Clara never expected Callie to release the man they both loved. And not for the reasons she told Jason that he later shared with her.

"OK, Jason. Let's just make sure that surprise is in Washington… not here on the interstate."

# # #

The Range Rover made the turn onto the country club drive that lead to the circular roundabout to the clubhouse front door and valet. As they passed the parking lot, Chase looked at the cars already there to assess their appeal and value. He noted a new McLaren parked in a special, well-protected slot that his Maserati did not qualify for. Next to it was a newer Aston Martin. At that moment, Callie's one-hundred-thousand-dollar SUV began to feel inadequate. When he handed the key fob to the valet, Chase did not make eye contact with the tip-enriched college boy. He was embarrassed that Callie's Range Rover did not measure up to the other vehicles in the high-end parking at the golf club.

Chase's recollection that Jason could be attending the rehearsal dinner made him nervous as they entered the club's private dining room that hosted the smaller dinner. Jason was from out of town and not part of the wedding party. If he were to attend, he would either be there waiting or make a noticeable entrance when he did arrive.

As they entered the dining room, Chase noticed the wedding party was not there. His look to the bar for relief said he would have to wait. They were just completing their set-up. Chase then moved to position away from the door and any possible interaction with Callie's former love. He moved to the window to watch a foursome play in on eighteen to finish their round for the day.

Callie felt relief as she watched Chase detach as he shifted toward the window. She looked around at the lavish decorations in the room that included three large, framed picture boards on three-legged easels. The one on the left focused on Sandy's daughter Maddie, as a baby, a growing child, and as a young adult. On the right was an identical presentation of Maddie's soon-to-be husband, Ramon, his family, and pictures of him as a baby, a growing child, and young adult.

Sitting between the two photo histories was the centerpiece presentation of photographs of Maddie with Ramon as college students, dating and when they were engaged. A picture of Maddie with Ramon was eerily similar to a picture of Callie and Jason that Callie's mother had saved. That photograph was taken just after their engagement was announced. It was a happy, fall photograph when their faces were still tan and their expressions were lit with the excitement of being together. Callie lost herself in Maddie and Ramon's picture as she replaced them with much younger, and happier, Callie and Jason.

"What's so captivating?" Chase asked while offering a glass of rosé.

Callie returned to the present to accept the glass of wine. Its cool temperature calmed her warming face from her recollection.

"It's just neat to see kids grow to adults, find each other, and get married," she answered.

"Well, I hope our kids make the right choices," Chase added while scanning through the pictures. "This is kind of cheesy."

Callie felt pressure hit her chest. His comment centered on the potential to miss-step, which she inferred he was saying about them. He also just insulted her best friend along with something that Callie thought was heartwarming and lovely for the evening.

"I still believe in love," she said watching his eyes shift from the pictures to her. "And I love these pictures."

"Then I do too, sweetie," he replied condescendingly with a soft, emotionless kiss.

As he pulled away from her, he touched the picture board lightly then turned to see who had arrived. A few unfamiliar guests were waiting for drinks by the bar. He motioned to Callie to walk with him as he moseyed over to welcome them until the hosts arrived.

# # #

Clara was asleep as Jason navigated through the traffic in northwest Washington, DC. As congested as the tight roads could be, the cars moved well in a coordinated chaos through the intersections and turns. Jason lived in the district for a short while to fill a year while applying to graduate business school. He spent his summer weekends riding his bike around the monuments, past the White House, and around the Capitol Building. The nice thing about Washington, DC, he thought, was despite all the constant building and renewal, the important landmarks stayed the same and the streets never changed.

As he pulled up to the valet, Jason touched Clara's arm to wake her.

"We're here," he said softly.

Clara lifted her head as she opened her eyes to the elegance of the building in front of her. The building along with its ornamentation was special. Clara's eyes expanded at the one-hundred-and-eighty-degree view of elegance that was going to be their home for the weekend.

"Do we really have to go to the wedding?" she asked, excited to be there.

"Yes." Jason smiled. "But not tonight."

The valet swept away both the luggage and Jason's car before they were on the stairs to the lobby. Clara walked slowly, mesmerized by the fine presentation of the public area. The lobby was rich with marble floors and walls. The furniture was suited for well-appointed living rooms. Clara thought back to her days with Marriott in Atlanta. This would have been a destination job for her. The perfect, final, professional landing spot to say you had made it to the top.

When they arrived in their room, their bags were already there. Jason took a moment to look around to ensure everything he ordered was in place. A bottle of champagne was chilling in a pewter champagne stand filled with ice. Two flutes were placed neatly on linen napkins on the table nearby. Clara took a moment to study the furnishings, touching each one to see if it was both real and to the quality she expected. She was not disappointed.

Jason pulled the bottle of champagne from its stand and worked its cork free as Clara continued to tour the suite. A loud pop of the cork startled her to a giggle as she turned to watch Jason struggle to pour the foaming wine into its waiting flutes. Successful, he lifted both flutes and walked to the window.

"Come here," he said.

Clara pushed some hair from her face as she walked to the window. The tenth-floor elevation gave a clear view of the vista Jason had reserved for their stay. To the left she could see the Washington Monument begin to glow in the fading sunlight. Just to the right, she could see the White House. The view was magical and spiritual. Clara could feel a pull to want to be in DC as more than just a visitor.

"This is unbelievable," she said, still entranced by the view.

"The scenery is beautiful," Jason answered, waiting for her to turn.

"Amazing, is more like…"

As Clara turned to him, she realized he was not talking about what was outside of the window. He toasted his flute to her with a smile. He had obviously seen the scenery outside their window before because his eyes, and complete focus, rested on her. The casual Southern girl with the great education and upper-class hospitality experience was radiating in the glow of the district's finest accommodations and the world's most powerful address at sunset.

"Ohhhh, take me to bed right now." Clara laughed as she leaned into him.

"Come on," Jason said, waving her back into the room. "I made eight o'clock reservations at the Old Ebbitt Grill. It's not the finest dining here, but it is some of the most historic."

Clara and Jason took their time to enjoy the champagne. Uncertain of what the night's dining would be, Clara was prepared with a variety of outfits suited for fine dining all the way down to a food truck. Jason's quirkiness gave no indication of what to expect. His answers to her questions before they left were frustratingly vague. Now she knew why.

Jason changed into a preppie outfit of heavy cotton khakis topped by a freshly pressed blue Polo Oxford button-down and sport coat. His horn-rimmed readers that he carried were going to complete his outfit that was perfectly suited for a casual Capitol Hill dining experience. Clara appeared in a dark, flowing, silk dress topped with a long-sleeved blouse and matching jacket. With her hair pulled back, her classic look, and the way her clothes moved as she did, gave Jason pause to just watch.

"Is this going to be OK?" Clara asked as she tilted her head with a smile.

"How could it not be?" he responded. "You're... perfect."

Clara swirled to pick up her glass from the table. As she took her last swig from the flute, she bumped up into Jason to give him a kiss.

"Thank you for making this so very special."

Jason looked befuddled as he searched for the right words to say. Humor was his usual go-to when the pressure was on.

"This? Pffft." He laughed.

Clara put her fingers to his lips to stop him.

"Just shut up for once. This is truly... lovely."

4

Chase finished his second bourbon as the wedding party started to arrive. His count excluded the dresser he had with Callie at home. He was about to move for his third when a flurry of groomsmen and bridesmaids arrived and headed straight to the bars to get their first alcohol of the night. Callie met Sandy and her husband Tom as they entered the room with Maddie's future in-laws. She looked for Chase as she was being introduced. Maddie and Ramon were waiting to make their own entrance that would be the center of attention and receive a roaring round of applause.

Chase circled the room to get in line for another drink as he observed the room. He realized, at some point, he was facing paying for three of these events. As he watched the bartenders hit a feverish pace to stay with demand, Chase felt thankful that two of his three children were boys. And that his bar bill for a rehearsal dinner, that is both smaller and shorter in time, would be far less than a full-blown wedding reception. He also knew the savings through his two boys would be reallocated by Callie to give her the resources she needed to give their only daughter, Lizzie, the fairytale wedding Callie would envision.

Looking around at the amenities of the room and club, Chase began to feel that the club was inadequate for what Callie would want for Lizzie. It was the place all of her friends would use to host their children's weddings. To have a wedding reception there would be ordinary. As he thought about alternatives, The Willard in the District came to mind as a premium place to host Lizzie's future wedding, complete with over-the-top elegance and walkable suites and rooms for guests. A wedding at the Willard would be the envy of everyone they knew and invited.

"Chase, Sandy and Tom are here. Please go say hello," Callie ordered. "Be social, for God's sake."

Callie knew Chase could work any room as well as anyone. His campaign work to befriend and manipulate support and donations to his clients built his reputation and success. Chase toasted his empty highball glass to acknowledge the order as well as to show why he was going to stop at the bar first before heading over to be social.

"Chase," Callie implored. "Don't get drunk tonight."

"No worries, sweetie," he replied. "I'm good with everything and anything tonight can throw at me."

Callie's heart dropped with that declaration. Chase had a history of using bourbon to loosen up, but he typically had the good sense on when to stop. The couples attending this rehearsal dinner were Maddie's and Ramon's families, along with out-of-town guests. Callie and Chase were invited as friends, who were also club members, to ensure that guests were well attended and able to find what they needed and wanted. Ramon's parents were funding the entire party, using Sandy and Tom Worth's membership. The entire event had to be executed perfectly.

"Chase," Callie said while taking his arm. "I want you to meet Sandy's brother Mark. He and his wife just arrived from London."

Chase turned, expecting to look eye-to-eye with Mark Fisher. He was surprised when he had to look up from his five-foot-ten-inch position to a towering six-foot-five man in a two-thousand-dollar suit looking down at him.

"This is my husband, Chase," Callie said as Chase slowly extended his hand to greet Sandy's brother. "Chase, this is Sandy's brother, Mark."

"I've known your wife for my entire life," Mark said a rich, deep voice consistent with the rest of his presentation.

"Mark was like my brother..."

"From another mother," he finished with her while laughing.

"Yeah, well, it's very nice to meet you," Chase droned, unamused by the humor.

"Sandy's told me a lot about you," Mark added. "You live a very interesting life. Your work certainly throws you into the middle of some big-time shit."

Chase digested each word for its apparent and true meeting. *He knows*, was the only thing that started running through his head as he listened. Chase smiled as he took a drink to fill time. The water from his melted ice reminded him that he was out of bourbon.

"You need a drink," Mark stated. "Let's you and I get our lovely wives a refill."

Mark extended his arm to direct Chase toward the bar. He smiled to both Callie and his wife Jen before heading off into the growing crowd. The crowd around the bar had thinned as guests started looking for their tables and dinner.

"So, you're Sandy's younger brother?" Chase asked to assess how this guy fit into her family and Callie's life.

"Older," Mark answered. "Five years older. So, they were nuisances I was charged with protecting. Callie didn't have any brothers. So, I guess, I was her closest to it."

The *brother* reference did not click with Chase. If Mark had been such a protector of Callie, they would have met. At a minimum, he would have heard stories about him.

"I'm sorry, but have we met before?" Chase started, a bit annoyed and just intoxicated enough to be borderline rude. "Were you at my wedding?"

Mark accepted his glass of cabernet and pinot grigio from the bartender before answering. Chase's drinks were delivered at the same time and remained on the bar as he asked.

"No," Mark answered. "I wasn't invited. When you two got married, I was on Callie's persona non grata list. Her shit list, so to speak."

The combination of the two phrases brought back the memory of Jason's congratulations to him at the restaurant when his divorce from Callie was imminent and Jason was in the driver's seat to win Callie back. It was the time he did take Jason's position as number one on Callie's family's shit list. A position he was not sure whether he ever surrendered.

"You're a friend of Jason Cartwright," Chase stated in a solemn tone.

"Best friends. Still are," Mark added while looking to locate their wives. "I was collateral damage when their engagement broke."

"So, what's this all about?"

Chase let his drinks sit on the bar as he squared to Mark. In his head, he could see Jason's six-foot-four-inch frame next to Mark's very fit, six-foot-five presence.

"Nothing really," Mark answered.

"Good. We should get back."

Chase turned to grab his two wines to head back for dinner.

"Well, maybe just one thing," Mark added as he looked to ensure no one could hear. "Let's just get one thing straight. You go at it with him... you go at it with me. And, with all that shit you pulled in your marriage with my honorary little sister, I won't just push your face into the sand."

Chase stood frozen as Mark made his position known. Having two red wines in his hands gave him the perfect opportunity to throw them in his face, to be followed by some punches to knock him back. The alcohol in him was advocating to do it. Mark's unsolicited threat, he felt, was real and imminent. There was forethought to it. He began to wonder if Jason and Mark had discussed the same vision of pummeling him at some point over the weekend as he had thought of doing to Jason.

"Don't fucking threaten me, man," Chase replied quietly, trying to not show any nerves.

"Just behave tomorrow—check that—for the rest of your marriage too, and we'll be good."

Mark nodded to indicate their discussion was over. He then turned from Chase to see the girls waving for his attention. As he navigated his way through the tables, he gave Sandy a quick smile and nod to say message delivered. Chase took time to grab some unneeded bar napkins to delay his walk and arrival. He then took the long way around the table to avoid any additional contact and to pick a chair opposite Callie's protector.

"It looked like you two had a mild disagreement," Callie observed with concern.

"Yeah," Mark laughed. "I jokingly told him I was an ardent Democrat. Chase wanted to debate it."

"Mark!" Jen laughed. "Forgive him. He thinks that's funny."

Callie saw the same joking in Mark that would be there with Jason. She also knew he was an ardent Conservative. His excuse was a lie.

The friendship between the three of them was influencing Mark's protective nature. She now knew he knew either some or all of her recent story with Jason and Chase. Sandy knew everything and could have shared it with him. As Chase remained silent and fiddled with his napkin, Callie looked to find Sandy looking back at her. Her expression showed relief that the first defensive strike was successful.

"Well, I'm sure he's taken much worse on the campaign trail," Callie joked nervously, using her wine glass to hide her concern.

# # #

The Old Ebbitt Grill was on the same block and walkable from

The Willard. The spring air had a warm dampness to it that felt heavy. There was a political tension and energy in the air that both Jason and Clara could feel. The establishment they were about to enter was wrought with history. Although relocated in 1985 from its original location, the Old Ebbitt Grille hosted politicians for decades as they dined and worked deals over drink and food. The setting was intoxicating, as if stepping back in time in political history to what politics was before streaming news and social media.

The building front was old limestone with the restaurant name embossed outward in the stone. The brass-framed glass doors were elegant and heavy to open. Jason held the door as he nodded for Clara to lead the way. Clara pushed her hair back as she smiled at him. Her dress flowed behind her like a flag waving in a light breeze. Jason loved her look and enthusiasm as he watched her wisp into one of the power centers of Washington.

"You are going to get so lucky tonight," Clara whispered as he pushed in her chair.

"I don't know if there is a measure that high," he answered with a light kiss on her cheek.

"This is really cool, and so me," Clara said while still studying her surroundings. "I could get used to this again."

Jason smiled as her enthusiasm to be in a big city again flowed from her. He thought of the way she looked on the first day they met when he arrived at Fox Farm to survive Christmas without his kids. His next thought recalled the relief she showed when they came to their agreement for him to buy the farm. But his best memory was of Clara after he pulled her under the water at the farm. He continued to smile as he visualized Clara completely soaked and covered in pond debris. His smile dropped as his eyes sank to the table when he remembered that it was also when Callie reappeared, looking for him. The magic of his first big-city night with Clara was disappearing with each new memory. It was then furthered by anxiety that was building in him because he and Callie were going to see each other again within twenty-four hours.

"Hey!" Clara said while giving him a soft poke. "I don't know what you're thinking about, but don't you ruin this for us."

As Jason's expression recovered from sadness to a pushed smile, Clara lifted her glass to toast the night.

"To us. To loving the same things. And to loving each other."

Her words and sentiment brought a full smile to his face as he raised his glass to meet hers.

"To love," Jason repeated.

Their water glasses met with a soft clink. As each took their sip, Jason withdrew back into his elevated anxiety.

"Come on, old man. Let's just eat, drink, and get lucky," Clara proposed, showing her concern at Jason's funk.

The invitation worked to pull Jason back to her. Clara knew that Callie was weighing heavy on him. Her hope that it was just his worry to protect her. Or that his concern was likely having to deal with Callie's bastard husband who could be unruly and provocative. But, deep down, Clara knew that his feelings for Callie would never sever. Just like her feelings for Tom, her ONE. She knew Tom would be able to pull her back if he ever rose from the dead. She knew that Callie had that same connection with Jason. And she was still alive and on course to be with him tomorrow.

As their drinks arrived, Jason lifted his iceless, Roughrider bourbon to celebrate the hard-ass legacy of Teddy Roosevelt it represented.

"Let me make a toast," he said with renewed vigor. "To the divine intervention that brought us together to save Fox Farm; AND to the divine INSPIRATION that was instilled in you to drive my car, and my sweet brown dog, seven hours just to let me know that you thought I was sexy."

Jason smiled as he watched Clara's face light then show disappointment with his finish.

"You saved me, Clara Haigh," he whispered to bring her back. "I thank God for you every day."

Clara smiled as she reached to touch his arm.

"That's so sweet," she replied, using the exaggerated Southern accent he loved. "Ditto."

5

"Saint Maria Goretti Parish," Jason read with a stumble as he waited for his light to turn green. "The patron saint of forgiveness."

"That's an odd name for a church," Clara remarked as she studied the sign.

"More like ironic," Jason answered, knowing that if this was Sandy's church, it was also Callie's and Chase's.

Saint Maria's had a stop light at its entrance to control crossover traffic access and egress to its campus and parking lots. Its exit had two lanes. The road that delivered worshippers from both directions expanded to three lanes in front of the church property to provide a turning lane. From the light, Jason could see a large white cross sitting on top of a contemporary building of sharp lines, wood beams, and complementary right-triangle stained-glass motifs that sat under the cross and above the sanctuary's two massive oak front doors. The church was similar to Callie's church in Cleveland. However, it was the polar opposite to her parents' church in Williamsburg.

Both Clara and Jason remained quiet as they studied the landscape while driving through the short wooded area that opened to the bigger campus of the church, its offices, and its kindergarten through sixth grade elementary school. The design of the campus road gave few options for parking other than with the crowd. Jason followed those in front of him and took the next available spot when it was his turn to park.

The lot was about half full when they started their walk toward the church. Clara watched as bridesmaids were delivered to the front door. Their shoeless runs into the building reminded her of her time as both a bridesmaid and a bride. She also saw a group of groomsmen huddled to the side of the building in a small sitting area, laughing and adjusting each other's ties. There was a crazy happiness in the air that was electric and soothing. She smiled at the thought that Jason was going to face something like this four times. She felt his hand take hers, then squeeze. He wanted to assure her he was there for her and that everything would be all right.

"This will be fun," he said as he glanced toward her.

Clara smiled at the comment. But her eyes showed concern for the uncertainty of being in a place she did not know, around people she had never met, and heading into what she expected had the potential to be really unpleasant.

"It WILL be fun," she replied. "And beautiful."

As she watched Jason continued to scan the crowd, a large hand took hers. A like presence then swept in beside her to walk in cadence with them. Startled, Clara turned to see an unknown tall man smiling back at her.

"Mark," he said as he looked to Jason.

Jason stopped when he heard the sound of Mark's voice. His face lit with a smile as his eyes teared and his grasp of Clara's hand ended.

"Dude," he proclaimed.

The slap of their hands, followed by the thud of their chests colliding, followed by a hug with hand slaps on their backs, said the two men knew each other. Jason, still smiling, pushed the man back, then looked to Clara.

"Well, that worked better than I expected," Jen said as she strolled in from behind to hug Jason.

"This is so awesome." Jason beamed, still staring.

"Clara," Clara interjected as she extended her hand to Mark.

Mark smiled as he studied Clara's demeanor to gauge her approachability. Noting a smirk in her expression, he decided to hug her. Clara accepted Mark's hug with a laugh. She was excited to meet an obviously positive side of Jason's history that was not a former love interest.

The ensuing introductions went well as Jason introduced Clara to Mark and Jen. Jen apologized for her husband's haunting, then gregarious approach to meeting her. Clara understood, better than Jen would ever realize, because Jason would have acted the same way. Their boys were cut from the same cloth. The concern shared by both Clara and Jen was the potential trouble the two could find through the course of an otherwise dignified event.

"I'm so glad you're here," Mark said to Jason as the four continued their walk to the church.

"This is a big day for your family," Jason replied as he put his hand on his friend's shoulder. "Family sticks together."

Clara and Jen exchanged glances and smiles as the boys continued their re-bonding. Their nonverbal communication was clear. The day, which was starting with a four o'clock wedding followed by a full country club reception through the evening, was going to have its moments to remember.

# # #

Callie noticed Mark and Jen pass by the church window, then turned back to her charges. Her job, which came with a bullet-pointed list of details and actions from Sandy, was to wrangle the bridesmaids to ensure their compliance with all the wants of the bride and all the restrictions of the bride's mother. Callie's role of demanding house mother kept Sandy in the most positive light for her daughter, the wedding party, and anyone who was watching and cared.

Jason and Clara were behind Mark and Jen but not seen by Callie. The two couples separated at the back of the sanctuary.

Sandy assigned Mark and Jen to sit with the family. Their elderly mother and father were attending to see their first grandchild marry. His responsibility was their safe and timely delivery to the family pew. They were scheduled to arrive with Sandy and the bride, to keep them involved in the special day. It was also to keep them as comfortable as possible.

The bridesmaids' room, later to be the bride's, was to the left of the large front doors to the sanctuary. On the opposite side was a coat and storage room. It also hosted the stairwell to the basement, where meeting rooms and the men's and women's restrooms were located.

The door to the bridesmaids' room was supposed to remain closed to allow the girls to make final wardrobe adjustments and to finish the finer points of their makeup. But the ins and outs of the ten bridesmaids made the needed privacy challenging and was driving Callie crazy.

As she reached to close the door again, Callie stopped the heavy wooden door from swinging shut when the sight she was nervous to see walked in from outside. Callie's chest tightened as she looked at him dressed in his traditional khakis and white, open-collared, buttoned-down shirt. His clothes were all starched and pressed to perfection. His navy-blue blazer hung beautifully and presented a nice sheen from being freshly cleaned. His Cole-Hahn cordovan loafers shined as if new. Jason's finished look, with his slightly gelled salt-and-pepper hair, was GQ. His entire presentation would have been perfect had he not been wearing dark, patterned socks. She forgave that indiscretion because it was still before Memorial Day. And he was Jason.

Time stopped for Callie as she watched Jason patiently wait to be escorted to a bride's side pew. Sandy never told her if he had responded as either a single or with a plus-one. She probably felt that both options would have been a problem for Callie. Single would have left him open for thoughts to approach him, which would not have been fair to either of them. A plus-one would mean that Jason had, at least for the moment, found someone new. That would have been a weekend spoiler too. Sandy knew Callie and Chase were still too dicey to add more stress to either of them.

As Jason continued to wait, Callie ran through memories of their time together during their first fall weekend, and again last summer. A smile came to her face as tears began to appear in her eyes. A wedding was where she should have been joined with him, not regretting that they were apart.

A touch on her shoulder told her that a bridesmaid had to leave. As Callie opened the door, a shriek filled the room as arms flew up and girls bunched together. The shriek echoed through the front hall area and into the sanctuary. A roll of soft laughter returned as people looked to see what happened. As Callie worked to control the youthful hysteria in front of her, she saw Jason looking back at her with a smile and that Clara was standing next to him. Callie noticed that she was holding his hand. And that her expression showed no happiness to see Callie.

Callie's first instinct was to wave, then close the door to focus back on the bridesmaids and to prepare for the incoming bride. It would have made the first sighting easier. But before she could flex a muscle to start the process, Jason was walking toward her with Clara still holding his hand.

"Hey," he said softly as he released Clara's hand to hug her.

Callie responded awkwardly, uncertain if it was a good idea to hug him. As she felt his arms close around her, his familiar musk flowed to her. She could not help but return his affection. Her embrace was soft and tender. It differed from the hard pull she used to put on his shoulder. A pull that inflicted a pain that he used to cherish until now.

"Hey," she replied with only a glance.

Her eyes looked down and off to the side as she gathered the courage to look at him. She knew that if she looked up, she would see him with another woman. A woman he was attached to beyond just a friendly relationship. Callie knew Clara ran one of his companies. She also knew she could not look away forever.

"Hi, Clara," Callie said as her eyes shifted to her. "It's great to see you two here."

Jason appreciated Callie's lie. Her true feelings showed on her face. She was not only struggling with the sight of him, but with him and Clara as a couple.

"It's nice to see you too," Clara replied.

The conversation quickly stopped between the three as each stood awkwardly looking at each other, then away. Each showed that they had thoughts running in their heads they could not say. Their expressions also showed that they all wanted to find an exit but were afraid to be the first one to break away. As Jason was about to speak, he saw Callie's eyes shift to the main door. Her look of pain made both Jason and Clara turn to see why she reacted that way.

The image of Chase standing frozen while looking back at them appeared as if he was under a spotlight. The fear in his face looked like they had caught him doing something bad. He was frozen where he stood, thinking about what he should do. He was stuck. To walk away would show weakness that he would not show Jason Cartwright. Chase decided to approach the three in the same manner he would stand up to a political opponent he could not avoid. His approach would be distant, but cordial.

"Jason," Chase mumbled as he arrived.

"Chase," Jason replied. "Let me introduce Clara Haigh. This is Callie's husband, Chase."

Clara clamped her lips to keep from smiling as she shook his hand. Her first impression matched what she had been told. His handshake was cold and limp. But she was still happy he was there. His look and swagger aligned with the cheater reputation he had. But it was also the reason why she was going to make love to Jason that night, and Callie was not. Clara scanned Chase's physique, noting the extra pounds, Gucci loafers, and no socks. Her overall impression was that he was a throw-back. Callie could do better. She and Callie both knew it because both of them had been with the same better.

"It's nice to meet you," Clara said, adding some juice to her Southern accent.

"You too," Chase answered.

As Clara let go of Chase's hand, Sandy appeared through the doorway with the bride. At that point, all four of them realized it was time to separate. Callie was to help Sandy settle and get Maddie finished for her walk down the aisle with her dad. Chase had to sit in his preassigned seat in the pew behind the family where Callie would join him. Jason and Clara turned to get one of the final escorts before the service started.

As Callie closed the door to the bride's holding room, she paused for a moment to look one last time at Jason and Clara. They were waiting for a groomsman to show them where to sit. Clara was laughing as she bumped into him playfully. His response was as she remembered him doing with her. He smiled adoringly, hugged her, and gave her a light kiss on the forehead. Clara's response was the same shy smile Callie used to playfully use to egg Jason on. Callie's heart was breaking again.

#

The congregation was seated and began to calm as the altar sat empty. A low murmur of conversation flowed through the sanctuary as friends and families conversed with each other.

Jason took Clara's hand as he studied the interior architecture of St Maria Goretti Parish, which reminded him of St. Matthew's in Cleveland. That was where his wedding with Callie was to happen. It was a place he had never visited prior to the day he and Callie met the priest who was to marry them. It was part of the process to declare their desire to get married. It was also where the requirement that, if married in the Catholic Church, their children would be raised in the Catholic faith was first presented.

The similarities of St Maria's to St Matthew's brought back the unpleasant feelings from that experience. It also brought back the required couple's weekend that proved its metal to throw a wedge between the two of them on the 'how should we raise our children' question. In hindsight, raising their children Catholic should not have been the issue it became for them. Allowing that debate to contribute to their separation was a haunting regret for Jason through his married life. He often wondered if Callie ever felt the same way.

Callie hustled down the center aisle, panicked to be seated before the music started playing. Being on bride's side enabled Jason to easily locate Chase. It also provided a clear line of sight to Callie. As she settled, Callie greeted people around her while doing a casual search behind her. When they locked eyes, Callie smiled briefly, then turned to face forward.

A string quartet that was nested to the left of the altar stairs started with a soft Pachabel – Canon in D. The music started as the priest and altar boys appeared. They were followed by the groom, his best man, and his nine groomsmen. All eleven were dressed in tailored navy-blue suits, white collared shirts, and ties to designate who was whom. The groom and best man wore ties that were different from the groomsmen's ties. The groom's tie had a delicate pattern of red, green, and gray. The best man's tie was a deeper garnet base with a light pattern. The groomsmen's ties were navy and carried the same light pattern. All eleven men wore small white lapel corsages.

As the music elevated, the bridesmaids walked down the aisle, properly spaced and stepping perfectly to the pace of the music. Sandy had the procession timed to the length of the music. As long as each bridesmaid held to the spacing and the pace of the music, the final steps of the final bridesmaid would coincide with the final slides of the quartet's bows across their strings.

Clara could see in Jason's face that he was a million miles away as the music played. She was used to his periodic tune-outs when, whatever was important at the time, would either put him in a trance or pull him from conversations they were having. She knew there was a lot that could be going through his head. And as much as she would have preferred it to be stressing over his four daughters getting married, she knew he was somewhere else thinking about Callie.

As the string quartet ended, Clara squeezed his hand to pull him back. She watched as the light appeared back in his eyes. When he looked at her, he knew he had been caught. He squeezed her hand and bumped his shoulder to hers to lighten the mood. His response gave her peace that whatever had happened up until then had not affected his feelings for her.

The high pitch of the organ that called for the congregation to rise rattled the glass in the windows and startled most of the people in the congregation. A soft laughter resulted as everyone rose and turned to face the rear of the church. Standing still in the back was the bride and her father. It was their time of reckoning. It was also the time that Jason envisioned Callie being the bride waiting to marry him before he chickened out.

As everyone turned, Callie was now behind Jason with the same clear line of sight he had to her. She noticed how well he and Clara stood together. Their hands were below what she could see. But the coordinated movement in their arms said they were connected. The room went silent as Callie watched Jason and Clara playfully stand in anticipation of the bride's procession. They resembled two twenty-year-olds. They were a lot like Jason and Callie when they first started dating.

The start of the bride's procession march brought Callie back to the moment. Maddie was glowing with excitement. Tom did his best to hold a dignified expression, all the while looking to explode in tears. Callie looked to find Sandy, two rows in front, with her parents. Her two sons were groomsmen. They were younger than the others and fidgeting on the end.

Sandy's face showed angst, as if worried that something would go wrong when everything had been planned to go right. Sandy could feel Callie's eyes on her and looked at her to give a quick smile. The single touch between the two best friends brought relief to her. Her face released its tension to radiate its usual warm, loving smile that said she was now enjoying what she had envisioned.

As the bride passed Jason and Clara's pew, they pivoted with her to watch the finish of her march to her waiting fiancé and the priest who was waiting to marry them. Jason watched Callie as she focused on the bride and her father. There was a glow in her eyes that appreciated the majesty of the moment. It was obvious that she was looking forward to her turn as the mother of the bride. He smiled as he watched Callie treasure the moment.

Before Maddie reached Callie's pew, Callie glanced at Jason to catch him watching her. A warm wash flowed over her face as she smiled back. They were having the same thoughts, what-iffing the bride they were watching was the daughter they never had. Callie's brow then furrowed as she turned back to watch Tom hand Maddie off to her fiancé, Ramon.

Tom's response, which he had practiced many times, that he and Sandy were giving Maddie away, trembled with emotion half-way through it. Jason felt, for the first time, the raw emotion of letting a daughter go. As his eyes teared, he felt Clara's hand tighten on his as her body leaned into him for support. She knew where Jason's head was at that moment. He needed to know she was there for him. And as they sat for the service, she did not let go.

6

Jason's ex-wife Stephanie was raised Catholic. Although Jason was a casual Presbyterian, they would go to Christmas and Easter services at her family's church. His general observation on religion was that man had distorted God's true intentions. That only the simplest, common threads from each faith were what God wanted everyone's obligations to be.

As the congregation stood to move forward for communion, Jason watched Callie go with Chase to receive the wafer and wine that recognized Jesus' sacrifice for their sins. As he watched Chase callously flip the wafer into his mouth, he wondered why God cursed Callie with a man like him. Short of being a nun, Callie was one of God's most devout followers. Yet he cursed her with such a cancer for a spouse. Chase was her test of faith.

Jason would admit later that his recall of the wedding ceremony, after the holy communion, was limited. The first half was spent in his head thinking about his four daughters, their wedding days, and the pressure of doing it all with and through his ex-wife, Stephanie. For a brief moment, he let his imagination flow to him and Callie experiencing the wedding of the daughter they never had. It was a bittersweet vision as the imaginary joy was soon ruined by the realization that it was just a dream. A dream that would never happen.

As the wedding service ended, Jason spent most of his thoughts on Chase, his narcissistic unfaithfulness, and Callie's courage to stay with him. It angered him to think that someone married to her, and who had children with her, could disrespect and treat her so poorly. His protective instincts began to boil as each thought passed. As Callie and Chase stood and followed the bride and groom's families up the aisle, Callie held Chase's hand and smiled as she walked by.

# # #

The string quartet that played at the church was in place and playing as Jason and Clara walked into the country club. The club entrance had an elegant presentation with a flagstone entry that melded into a marble floor. Periodic throw rugs were in place to soften the walk in and to the various rooms and venues. The quartet was situated perfectly in the near corner of the club's grand ballroom so that guests would be drawn to the music and the wedding celebration.

Jason recognized the four string players as he approached the ballroom. He started to wonder about how they could have vacated the church without notice to arrive and set up in time at the club. Moving themselves, with two large instruments, would have created a stir in the church. He then realized that the communion commotion was their perfect opportunity to exit while everyone else stood and moved up to and away from the alter.

As they entered the ballroom, Jason picked up a folded card from an alphabetized display. The card was alphabetized to him and included Clara's first and last name as his plus-one. Inside were their assigned seats for dinner.

Jason noted that his assigned table number was low, indicating that he would be near the bridal table. He also looked to see Callie and Chase Larson's card still on the table. Curiosity was pulling him to look to know their table number. But, with Clara at his side, he did not want to appear distracted from her.

Great Falls Country Club's ballroom was large enough to comfortably host a three-hundred-person wedding dinner, a dance floor, four bar stations, and a band. The quartet was against the wall to the left of the first bar in the room. The bandstand and dance floor sat between the entrance and two bars and the dining tables.

Each dining table was decorated with a long, flowing tablecloth surrounded by eight cushioned chairs suited to a high-brow club event. Eight people per table enabled easy conversation between everyone. The bridal party sat at a long, elevated table that was front-and-center to the guest tables and just to the right of the bandstand.

The dance floor was hardwood. It was the original surface to the ballroom, eliminating the tripping hazard found in the temporary parquet floors some clubs and hotels used to create their dance areas.

Jason looked to see what the band would entail. The impressive drum set, keyboards, two stations with guitars, and a lead singer's microphone showed that the band was going to rock. The dance floor accommodated happy hour as people arrived and gathered. A few spills required cleanup during dinner to make the floor safe for dancing. Three sets of French doors were also open to an adjoining terrace overlooking the eighteenth green for people interested in fresh spring air before sitting down for dinner.

The devil in Jason thought it would be fun to request the song he and Callie first slow danced to on her first night at the beach with him. A smile appeared on his face as he thought through that moment and what he had to do to get the song requested and played. He never told Callie that he requested that song, although the tip paid through the high five he gave the lead singer should have been a strong indicator. Jason felt that it appeared better as a band choice that just happened to occur shortly after they arrived.

As the crowd continued to flow in and to the bars, Jason took Clara's hand to lead her through the maze of tables to find table number three and the closest bar to it. As expected, the table was to the left of the bridal party's long table that sat in front of everyone.

Jason left Clara to claim their seats with her purse and to wait.

He returned with a glass of chardonnay for her and his usual double bourbon, neat.

"This is an expensive wedding," Clara commented, recalling hers as far less opulent yet still expensive.

"Sandy comes from money," Jason replied while still looking around. "I'm sure Tom is a beltway bandit and rakes it in too."

Jason's cold, borderline rude comment to the source of their funds for the event startled Clara. It appeared as though he had a chip on his shoulder regarding easy money inherited versus having to go out and earn it. She watched his eyes close as he pulled his first taste of bourbon.

"If you all were best friends growing up, you're all are cut from the same cloth," she observed while watching him digest her question.

"You'd think. But that's not the case."

"So, Callie..."

"...was way above my station," Jason finished. "That was one of our issues."

Clara watched Jason work through the admission as he turned to face her. His face was absent of all emotion. This was a serious history fact he wanted her to know.

"So, she was concerned about you marrying her for her money?" she asked nervously.

Jason smiled at the question. It was the natural question given the situation.

"No," he answered, "to the contrary. She wanted to combine my money with hers to be ours. Her dad insisted it be that way."

Clara smiled at the problem she wished Tom had presented to her.

"So, what was the problem? People marry others just for their money all the time."

Jason moved his eyes from the ballroom to her. Clara's comment, although joking, was disconcerting. Jason was her white knight who saved her Fox Farm cabin business. For a moment, he wondered if the joke was showing her true motives to be interested in him.

"Not me," he answered coldly.

His tone was to end the conversation. Clara could feel his disdain for the topic. As she looked to find something else to discuss, Mark and Jen appeared, happy to see them standing near table three.

"Table three?" Mark asked, knowing that Sandy had placed the two couples together.

Jason smiled as he clinked bourbons with his best friend. Clara could see the anxiety drain from his face now that a better distraction had been placed in front of him. As the four settled into conversation, Sandy and Tom arrived with Sandy's two elderly parents to complete their table of eight. Jason and Clara were seated at the family table to celebrate the marriage of their only daughter, granddaughter, and niece to, hopefully, her ONE.

#

The time for dinner was not published. But Sandy had it scheduled to be served at 6:30 p.m. This provided just over an hour of happy hour where the bridal party could take pictures and guests could be seated for the introductions of the bridesmaids, groomsmen, best man, maid of honor, and the bride and groom. The evening was designed to be fun where the introduction of each bridal party member had a short personal biography to be read as they entered the party. Sandy required advance submission of the bios for editing, then secured them with the club manager to ensure they were kept clean.

As Jason introduced Clara to Sandy's parents, he saw Callie and Chase enter the ballroom by the quartet. Chase was holding their table card, squinting to read the number. He then started to look at each table's number to find his. Jason watched Callie follow behind Chase as he navigated through the crowd and tables. He was happy to see she was holding a glass of white wine, with a healthy club member pour, to start her evening.

Chase's eyes lit as his arms flew up to greet his friends at their table. Jason felt guilty knowing that his presence bumped Callie from the family table. A sacrifice she would have gladly made to place her wants and needs second to the higher good of a better wedding experience for Sandy, Tom, Mark, Jen, and Jason. Although Callie knew where Jason was seated, she did not look his way as she took her chair to say hello to the other wives as their men gathered together.

"So, you're facing four of these," Mark asked, knowing Jason was always running numbers in his head.

"Not like this," he answered. "My oldest has already stated she wants a destination wedding. My second has declared she's never getting married. I'm sure one of the last two will want something grand, like this. If I only knew then what I know now."

Jason took a pull of bourbon as he pondered the thought. Mark smiled to his confirmation that he had hit a nerve. He then patted his friend on the back to assure him everything would be OK and that he would be at each wedding.

"My daughter will probably marry a Frenchie." Mark laughed. "I don't know where that will happen. It'd be cool to have it in London, but…"

Mark nodded toward his parents as he finished the statement. It was clear that neither his mother nor father were in any condition to make a trip that far. Jason smiled to see the elderly couple enjoying their drinks as they observed the chaotic flow of youth on the dance floor. He would have cherished his parents seeing his daughters get married.

"Let's hope they get to see it," Jason answered, teary with sentiment for his opportunity for that to happen.

7

The dinner exceeded all expectations. The food choices were exquisite, and the execution of the food delivery was perfect. Clara watched the orchestration of the staff as items were delivered, then removed, in perfect cadence with the needs of each table. The bars remained open as wine was also poured for each guest at the table. The conversation and laughter throughout the room was elevating. Jason could see Chase holding court at his table, keeping the men in stitches as their wives rolled their eyes and talked privately.

The arrival and presentation of the wedding cake quieted the roar of the room down to a murmur. It was strategically timed to the finish of the main course's delivery to give the staff time to cut and ready dessert slices to be delivered after dinner ended.

Maddie and Ramon slowly approached the five-tier cake made for three hundred with smiles and a playful eye toward both the crowd and each other. Together they held the large, ornate knife to make the first cut of cake, followed by a round of applause and cheers. As the first slice was presented for its first taste, revelry started at the younger tables to entice them to smash the cake in each other's face.

As both took a pre-cut cube of cake and icing, they looked at each other with an eye-message to stick to their agreement not to mess the other's face.

To egg on the crowd, Maddie and Ramon took a dramatic pause to seek crowd permission to cake-smash their new spouse. Ramon was just about to violate his premarital promise when he looked to see Sandy glaring at him. Her message was clear.

If he wanted good relations with his mother-in-law, he was to gently feed cake to her perfectly adorned daughter. Both bride and groom complied with their original agreement.

A moan of disappointment followed by applause sounded as Maddie and Ramon both gently placed cake in the other's mouth. The sight reminded Jason of his final morning with Callie in October. They used Maya's left-behind doughnuts to simulate the same act. Their effort was less successful, leaving glaze on both of their faces. With the cake cutting completed, Maddie's dad, as father of the bride, stood to greet his guests and to toast the new couple.

Tom's toast was warm, funny, and emotional. His voice trembled several times as he worked to convey his love for his daughter, his wife, and their family. He welcomed Ramon's family, by individual name, into theirs with a brief funny story on their first meeting years earlier. He finished with a glowing tribute to Sandy's parents as well as to all the loved ones who were not there for any number of reasons. Sandy glowed as she watched her husband finish his toast. Jason smiled as he watched her wipe tears from her eyes before standing as Tom said his final words before handing the microphone to the best man. As he returned to the table, Sandy embraced her man, generating another round of applause from the guests.

Ramon's best man was feeling little pain as he fumbled with his paper notes. A growing laughter encouraged him to ham up his toast, which his inebriated state welcomed. The resulting toast, despite starting rockily, was well thought out, written, and executed. The young man showed moxie in front of the three hundred guests who were glued to his every word. His annunciation, timing, and delivery were all polished. Jason looked to Mark, who nodded back in agreement that the best man was a hit.

As the maid of honor stood to say a few words, Mark stood to make his way around the table. Jason looked to Jen, who shrugged her shoulders to what he was up to. Sandy took her eyes off the bumbling words of Maddie's maid of honor, who was just winging it, to watch her brother take a position behind her.

The crowd's applause was generous when Maddie's maid of honor finished her toast. Although challenged for clarity all the way through, her sentiment was sweet and her finish was memorable. Full of emotion, she was confused about what to do when she was finished.

Mark stepped up behind her and held his hand out to take her arm. Her delight to see him was apparent as she quickly surrendered the microphone and hurried back to her seat. Laughter gave Mark time to settle in. It also gave the maid of honor time to return to her seat and giggle with her friends.

"If I may," Mark started, then paused. "Most of you don't know me. But... I am Maddie's Uncle Mark. I live with my lovely wife Jen and our two kids in London. So, coming here for the wedding was an undertaking, to say the least."

The crowd began to settle as Mark spoke calmly.

"I just want to take this opportunity to talk about family. The whole purpose of a wedding is for two people that find each other to perpetuate and grow families through the generations with new love.... and offspring."

Mark paused to give the expected responses to children their due time.

"I look at my parents and marvel at the fact that they not only found each other, but that they loved each other for a lifetime, and, more so, that they survived ME, and my siblings, to be here today. And, believe me, we gave them a run for their money."

The crowd laughed to Mark's true representation and confession. Jason smiled as he thought of their childhood craziness while watching Sandy's parents shake their heads in agreement.

"So, with that history, sorry, sis, my thought is this."

Mark nodded to Sandy as he added a dramatic pause.

"To Maddie and Ramon, you are starting a remarkable journey of love that will lift your hearts to their highest capacity to love as well as test your patience to the deepest levels you can take. The secret is to share, to be open, and to contribute. Taking should be only for something that is given freely. The marvels of growing older together, raising children together, and just being together through it all, can't be described. I'm here, in person, from London, England, to celebrate the start of your journey together. And, I ask all of your friends and family—and I'm sure some are the same people—to raise their glasses with me to wish you all the best of everything that's yet to come."

Clara watched Jason as Mark finished his toast. The gravity of Mark's words struck her hard as they brought back memories of Tom, their courtship, wedding, and married time together. It brought back the sense of loss she felt from the time before he died until the day she and Jason coupled. Guilt piled on to that feeling as she thought about her regret to not think about him as regularly as she did just after he died. She took Jason's hand to feel a '*good*' to push away her pain and anguish.

The tears in his eyes showed Mark's words had touched Jason too. His line of sight to Mark had Callie's table in the background. Jason smiled, then turned to Clara as he felt her hand squeeze his. As she looked back to Mark, she noticed Callie looking over at them as Chase restarted the conversation at their table.

"Hey," Jason whispered.

Clara jerked as she stopped staring at Callie's table to look at him.

"Come back to earth. I'm the only one that's allowed to drift away."

Clara smiled to his words.

"Don't you dare," she replied with a smile, as Callie watched her kiss him.

# # #

The band exceeded all expectations and was true to the quality of the event and the facility. Their opening mix had enough to pull the younger guests onto the dance floor while giving the older crowd something to dance to. Maddie and Tom took the floor first to dance alone. The room stayed silent as the lights stayed dim to give them their time together. As the song ended, Tom escorted Maddie to Ramon, who danced with his bride through a slow, acoustic love song.

As their dance ended, the parents of the bride and groom joined their children to Louis Armstrong's "Wonderful World." Mark encouraged his parents to join the parent dance at their granddaughter's wedding.

As the song ended, the band paused to give the bride's grandmother and grandfather time to reach safety. When they were settled back at their table, the music amped up to a mix of oldies and new songs that everyone knew and enjoyed. The dance floor maintained a steady stream moving on, then off, then to the bar. The sound level, manageable through dinner, fast exceeded the levels for anyone to carry on a casual conversation at a table.

When Jen and Clara excused themselves to the ladies' room, Jason and Mark took the opportunity to move outside for some fresh air and an opportunity to catch up without their plus-ones.

"Want one?" Mark asked as he handed Jason a cigar.

"No," Jason replied. "And stand downwind from me if you're going to smoke that thing."

"There is no wind." Mark laughed as his lighter ignited and he started puffing plumes of smoke into the air.

"Let's move where you won't offend anyone."

The end of the terrace overlooking the golf course was empty, with room beyond it for Mark to exhaust the stink of his cigar. Tables and chairs were in place for guests. Each table had a lit candle. But the setting appeared to be part of the normal furnishings for the terrace.

"So, Clara, she's nice," Mark stated as he settled into his chair.

"Very pretty, Southern. You hooked a good one."

Jason smiled, then nodded in affirmation.

"She says our meeting was a mixture of divine intervention and inspiration."

Mark's expression shifted from humor to intrigue.

"There's got to be a story there," he commented. "And with all the shit you've been through with Callie too."

Jason paused as he showed surprise.

"How much do you know?"

Mark smiled as he extended both his hands out with palms up. His message was clear. He knew everything because Callie had told Sandy. And Sandy had told Mark.

"Dude, you've got a beautiful, smart, Southern woman with you who really seems to dig you."

"She is fantastic," Jason admitted.

"Love?"

Jason watched Mark's eyes zero in on his. A smile returned to his face as he both thought and pondered how to respond.

"Define 'love,'" he answered as Mark exhaled another plume of smoke.

"Come on, man," he implored. "Everyone can see how you're stuck on Callie. You couldn't keep your eyes off her during dinner."

"Well, the table planner should not have put her in my direct line of sight along with her party-boy, d-bag husband holding court."

Mark's expression dropped as Jason exhausted his frustration.

"She still looks good," Mark conceded.

"Looks, smells, tastes…" Jason added.

The last admission appeared to be new information as Mark's eyes opened widely. The revelation caused him to laugh.

"Oh my God," he chortled while wiping his eyes. "You are one fucking glutton for punishment."

The two childhood friends laughed in agreement to Mark's observation, then fell silent. Mark was a few drags short of finishing his cigar as Jason swirled what was left of his bourbon in his glass.

"Mark!" Jen called out from near the door.

The sound of his wife's voice and tone startled him to an upright position. He took one last pull on his cigar before extinguishing it in an ashtray and launching it out into the landscape. Jason smiled to what he knew was coming.

"At Fox Farm, we'd charge you fifty bucks for that cigar butt out there."

"I want to hear about that and your OBX place." Mark replied as he moved forward in his seat. "Sounds like we have some places to visit."

Mark and Jason stood as the girls arrived. Both men noticed their drinks were empty and in need of a refill. The music was also what Jason felt he could dance to without either embarrassing or injuring himself. As usual, in a very short timeframe, Mark had summed up his best friend's obsession with Callie as destructive. It was the same type of matter-of-fact observation he set forth when Jason was stressing and accepted the ring back from Callie twenty-eight years ago.

As the women got closer, Mark made an awkward attempt to wave the stink of his cigar away. Jen stopped and kept her distance as she waved her arms and hands to help move the stale air.

"Mark, really?" she asked, noting he was going to pay for his pleasure.

As Clara settled in next to Jason, she showed she was happy Jason did not cave to share Mark's nasty habit. An unexpected kiss on her cheek caused her to blush. Jason smiled and paused as he pulled back to reorient to her. The anxiety Clara felt through dinner as she watched Jason struggle with his emotions was released by that one little gesture. She took his hand to pull him back to the party where she could touch him more publicly on the dance floor to declare that he was hers.

# # #

The throwing of the bouquet always tormented Clara. She despised it as a single when attending her friends' weddings as either a bridesmaid or a guest. She hated when Tom would send her into the pile of women as a fun way to embarrass her.

As the band went on break, a hired master of ceremony stepped to the microphone to call for all available women to step forward for the bouquet toss. Clara knew the time was coming and tried to coordinate a bathroom run to the toss. It was only fair that the younger girls should catch the bouquet, not some old widow.

Jason held Clara's hand, smiling as he watched Maddie take hold of her bouquet. He knew that the better idea was to let Clara choose where to be when the toss happened and to not force her to participate. As the pool of more than twenty women under thirty-five gathered for the toss, he looked to Clara to gauge her interest.

Clara initially was looking to get Jason's agreement that not participating in the bouquet toss was OK. His smirk sent the message she wanted, but she also saw it as a dare to participate. Clara was looking for something out of character to do to excite him. As the MC made last call for all the single ladies, she released his hand to hustle to the dance floor. Her attention was on him as she quickly walked between the tables. Her movement caught the attention of the MC who waited for the eager older lady to arrive before nodding for Maddie to make the toss.

Callie was standing near the bandstand with Sandy as the countdown started. Her happy expression was forced as she watched Clara settle into the rear of the pack of available women. She glanced to Jason to see what he was watching. His face was lit with excitement as his eyes stayed focused on Clara. As he shifted from Clara to the bride, he noticed Callie watching him. A quick survey of the crowd did not show Chase in the room. When his eyes returned to Callie, she was focused on the last two counts to the toss.

The twenty-four-foot ballroom ceiling provided ample space for a high toss of the bouquet. The wedding photographer asked Maddie to intentionally toss it high so that he had enough time to rapid-fire pictures from the start to the finish. A high toss always resulted in a beautiful picture of the bouquet falling into a cluster of women with extended hands anxious to catch it.

"Holy volleyball set," Jason laughed as he watched the bouquet peak at about sixteen feet.

As predicted, when the bouquet started its fall, the pack of anxious women pressed together to create a floor of hands to grab the bundle. As it reached their fingertips, their collective jumps to catch it popped the bouquet back up into the air for a second fall. The women had to reset and move with the new direction of the flowers, which pressed back upon the rear of the crowd and Clara.

To show some effort, Clara held her hands high to be an engaged part of the group. The shift of the crowd caused the women around her to stumble toward her. Their resulting movement pushed Clara backward, causing her to fall to the floor on her bum. The bouquet then glanced off the collective hands of the crowd before landing in her lap. Mortified, Clara gently took hold of the flowers, slowly stood, then held them high in the air to declare victory.

The surrounding crowd roared with applause and cheers for both what happened and for Clara being a good sport to the outcome. As she looked around the room, she looked as Jason when she brought the bouquet down and pointed it at him. Her message was you owe me. Callie read it as staking her claim.

"She's a keeper," Mark laughed hysterically while wiping tears from his eyes.

Jason nodded to Mark as he applauded and walked to the side of the dance floor to give his embarrassed girlfriend a hug for comfort and support. The insanity of the bouquet toss made him forget what was coming next. Mark was relishing the thought of watching his best friend when his newest love interest had to accept the bride's garter from someone likely half her age.

8

While still enjoying Clara's impressive handling of the most awkward bridal bouquet toss, it did not occur to Jason that turn-about was fair play. So, when the Master of Ceremonies made the call for all available men, he remained next to Clara, clueless to that fact that he was one.

"Well?" Clara asked to tune him in to the call.

"You're kidding?" he replied. "Right?"

"Not only are you doing this," she answered. "You better kill to get it… I am not having some twenty-year-old work his way up my inner thigh."

Jason smiled to his marching orders, concerned about his ability to catch a garter. As the MC saw him emerge onto the floor, he made a special remark to the gentlemen coming out to keep what was his.

The removal of the bride's garter had the drama and laughter that usually happened when the groom approached his bride under the eyes of his father-in-law and three hundred other on-lookers. Jason, like Clara, stood toward the back of the pack. His memory of garter tosses was that enthusiasm and effort to catch it was always low. The odds of being victorious were enhanced by that fact, Clara's age, and the notably shorter group of men he was competing against.

The same instructions were given to Ramon by the wedding photographer. The best pictures come from tosses that arch high and fall into reaching hands. As Ramon worked his way to re-move Maddie's garter, Jason looked to Clara. She was standing next to Jen and Mark. Mark smiled with a thumbs-up to wish him luck. Jason wished he had downed Mark's bourbon before becoming part of the action. He then looked at Callie standing next to Sandy. Both gave endearing smiles to wish him luck against boys who could be dating his daughters.

The arch of the garter was high, like a long home run hit out of a baseball park. It climbed in altitude as it carried toward the back of the crowd. As it ran out of steam, it slowed then dropped quickly. As expected, the men in the crowd did not have the same vigor to win the prize as the women. Jason held his hand higher than theirs. Without leaping, he grabbed the garter before the others let it fall to the floor.

"This will be interesting," Chase remarked as he clapped.

He was anxious to have the rest of the ceremony play out in front of Callie, to reinforce the fact that Jason had found someone new and that she was stuck with him. He watched his wife stand with her best friend as the final act of the bouquet toss was about to happen.

Callie gave Jason a smile for support as a chair for Clara was placed in the center of the dance floor. Up for the challenge, and with just enough wine to accept the realization that she would never see anyone in the crowd again, Clara sauntered slowly to the chair while batting her eyes and finishing with a twirl before sitting down. Jason waited for his call before stepping forward. The playfulness between the two was enjoyed by the crowd as Callie watched. She kept a smile planted on her face, distracting herself from her sadness by concentrating to keep clapping.

The crowd roared when Clara kicked her foot up dramatically then called for Jason with a finger gesture. Not to be outdone, Jason took three fast steps across the floor, paused, then finished with three more to slide on his knee in front of her. His whimsical approach captivated Clara, and the crowd disappeared.
As Jason removed Clara's shoe, he ran the palm of his hand up her thigh. The sensation tightened her stomach, forcing her to

lean toward him. The feel of the garter slipping past her foot up onto her thigh sent a tingle through her body. His finish up and past her knee was slow, soft, and romantic.

As he put her shoe back on her foot, he reached to help her stand. Together they twirled to the applause and shouts of the crowd. At the finish, Jason kissed Clara lightly on the lips before ending with a twirling hug neither of them thought anyone saw.

As they separated to exit the floor, Clara's consciousness returned to the party to notice the crowd again. Her face turned red as she raised the bouquet to shield her embarrassment. Jason gave Clara a curtain call by extending both his arms toward her. His smile sent the message she was waiting to hear.

They walked off the floor as the band started its second set.

# # #

"I would never embarrass you like that," Chase remarked as he stopped behind Callie.

"That was the most romantic thing I think I have ever seen."

"You would've hated every minute of it." Chase laughed with his eyes still on Clara. "You wouldn't have played her part that well either."

"You're such an asshole," Callie whispered at him before walking off.

# # #

The restrooms were set in a small alcove near the front door of the clubhouse. Sandy, Clara, and Jen were settled in at the table to talk and laugh about the bouquet and garter toss. Both feared that Clara was going to have to face an inebriated twenty-something stumble through both his intoxication and the embarrassment of putting a garter on someone near his mom's age. Jason set the three up with wine before heading to the restroom.

As he left the men's room to return to the party, he heard the band playing the slow song he requested on Callie's first night with him in October.

"This isn't a coincidence," she said as she stepped out from the wall.

"That's my favorite song."

"I know." She smiled. "I requested it. Just like you did."

Jason smiled to her admission.

"Then you'll need some cash to tip them."

Jason invited Callie to walk with him to see if Clara was still OK with Sandy and Jen. Still engaged in conversation, he moved to the side to be out of their sight and out of earshot of most of the guests.

"I'm sorry I'm here," he said as she settled close. "I'M REALLY SORRY for that scene with the bouquet and the garter."

Callie exhaled as she gave a slight smile.

"If Mark wasn't going to be here, I would have declined."

Callie's eyes drifted from his down to the floor as her smile disappeared.

"Seriously," he added to pull her back. "I'm sorry."

Callie paused to listen to his words before responding. She pushed her chestnut brown hair back behind her ear as she put thoughts together for him.

"You have to be here. Mark, Sandy, Mr. and Mrs. Fisher… they're all family to you."

"And you," Jason added.

Callie's head began to shake slowly back and forth as she looked into Jason's eyes.

"I'm sorry," she whispered while still shaking her head. "I'm so sorry that I started everything with you again. I'm sorry for last summer. I'm just—"

Jason grabbed Callie as she crumpled. Although in a corner, their location was still public enough to be seen. Country club grapevines have brutal histories of passing both true and untrue gossip about guests and other members. Jason escorted Callie down the hall and into an empty sitting room.

The sitting room was textbook country club. It had the hunt scene portraits on the walls, an oriental rug, and some elegant sofas and chairs that looked to be out of someone's rich grandmother's house. Callie sat on the loveseat near the door as she collected herself. Jason found some tissues in a chest of service items. His awareness of the wedding was gone as he focused on Callie's emotional breakdown.

"I thought, with all the drama of last summer, with Mom dying, Will's unbelievable comment about you and me, and Chase's obvious jealous attempt to win me back would make things different. But he's the same asshole I was divorcing before that all happened."

"I can have him killed," Jason joked, looking to release her tension. "Really, I know people. Mountain people."

Callie responded with a deadpan expression that just held. Jason tried to prod her to at least smile with a smile and some head tilts. After a few gestures, she released her stubborn need to resist and smiled.

"That bouquet and garter thing was the best I've ever seen," Callie whispered as she wiped her eyes. "Clara stayed so composed through the fall, then went for it afterwards. You... you with your stutter-step, shimmy-up thing and then sweeping onto your knee. It took my breath away. It was so romantic."

Jason put his hand on hers as she shifted her eyes to the ground.

"You two are awesome together," she finally admitted.

"It was all a show... for the crowd."

Callie started shaking her head to his lie.

"No, you two likely didn't even notice the crowd," she replied.

"You were off in your own little capsule millions of miles away."

Jason did not deny Callie's observation. To do so would not be fair. He reached to lift a small strand of hair that had fallen in front of her face to place it back behind her ear. As he finished, Callie took his hand and pressed it against her cheek.

"I miss you," she said, as he sat staring back into her tear-filled eyes.

"Me too."

Jason slid close to give Callie an awkward hug. Her hands touching his back were warming. Their time together was disturbing everything that settled back last summer. He knew the scenario that was rolling out was going to be troubling. But, for now, his focus was to comfort her until she could rejoin the party.

# # #

The moment his phone vibrated in his jacket pocket, he knew who it was.

Where are you? confirmed it.

Jason lost track of time as Callie dealt with, and admitted, she was wrong to not have listened to his warnings about Chase last summer.

"I'm sorry," he said. "Clara's looking for me. I can't leave her too long. She doesn't really know anyone here."

"That's fine," Callie answered. "I'm good now. Go ahead."

Jason stood to leave, expecting Callie would walk out with him. As she continued to sit, he became concerned about her well-being and sat back down.

"Callie, let's get you up and moving, maybe a cold glass of something to perk you back up."

As she began to stand, Callie grabbed his hand for stability. Her legs felt weak from her emotional breakdown. She walked slowly as they exited the room.

"Well, what do we have here?" Chase asked as he stumbled in from the ballroom.

"It's nothing, she's upset," Jason replied.

"What? A quickie for old time's sake wasn't good enough?" Chase retorted.

His bloodshot eyes said he was fully lit.

Jason grabbed and squeezed Chase's jacket lapel to stop his drunken assault on his wife's character. Chase did not resist the assault.

"Eaaasy, cowboy," Chase replied while bound tightly in his jacket. "You'd never get out of here if you think it's GO time."

Chase's squished face turned to a smile as he watched Jason process his words. Jason had to let him go, again. For his sake, and Callie's.

"Chase, you're drunk and embarrassing yourself," Callie inserted.

"I'm also still your husband, sweetie," he answered as he straightened his jacket and entered the men's room. "And the father of your children."

Jason phone buzzed again. Knowing it was Clara, he did not check its message. Chase's behavior, and his nearly hitting the breaking point to clobber him, had deepened Callie's emotional state. He needed to get her to Sandy, so that he could go find Clara.

#

The wedding reception closed in stages as the first wave of older guests left after the festivities and the younger guests waited out the band. Jason placed Callie with Sandy, who took care of her with Jen's help. Mark had surpassed his limit of bourbon and was sitting quietly on the patio smoking cigars. Jason and Clara finished the night on the dance floor and some moonlit conversation off by themselves, away from the party and absent of any mention of Callie.

"Mind if we join you?" Jason asked as he and Clara sat away from the cigar smell.

"That was one damn fine wedding," Mark declared. "Damn bar's closed, though."

"Give me your glass," Jason said while reaching toward him.

As Mark handed his glass to him, Jason pulled a full fifth of Woodford bourbon and barely touched bottle of Mondavi Reserve Chardonnay from beside his chair.

"I think the bar's going to have a short count tonight." Jason laughed as he filled their glasses.

"Good man," Mark answered as he accepted, then lifted his double pour to the light.

"Jesus Christ! You two," echoed from inside the ballroom as Sandy walked through with Tom. "I closed the bar thirty minutes ago."

"Well." Jason laughed. "That's odd, because I lifted these two bottles about fifteen minutes ago. Otherwise, we'd have nothing to drink."

Jason looked to Mark who smiled as Sandy, Jen, and Clara just shook their heads.

"I'll pay for it." Jason laughed again.

"Just wait, funny man," Sandy responded. "Let's see how excited you are when you get the bill."

#

Sandy smiled as she grabbed the Woodford to pour herself a double to celebrate the success of the wedding and reception. Jason filled everyone's glass to ensure readiness for his impending toast.

"To the mother of the bride… and Tom," he started. "For everything you did and have done up until today. Thank you for this wonderful time together. This has truly been memorable. We look forward to it continuing at brunch tomorrow, at your house."

Everyone raised their glass to celebrate Sandy's great achievement. Mark's suggestion that they try to push on through to morning and the brunch fell on flat ears. The party was ending and it was time to head home.

"I just wanted to come out to say goodnight to everyone," Callie said from the doorway, jealous to not be part of the revelry. "Chase and I had a wonderful time. Sandy, Tom, congratulations. We'll see everyone else at the brunch tomorrow."

As Callie waved goodnight, she scanned the faces in the group to make eye contact with everyone. Jason was on his feet and nodded as she held her gaze on him longer than the others. As she receded back through the doorway, he looked down at his friends whose eyes were all on him. Clara took his hand to remind him she was still there.

Chase paced anxiously around the clubhouse lobby as his Maserati sat at the door idling. Callie was nowhere to be found.

As Jason and Clara appeared to leave, Chase spun around, still intoxicated and quite angry that Callie was still a no-show to go home.

"Well, at least she's not with you," he said snidely as he continued to scan the area. "You staying at one of the hotels nearby?"

Jason exchanged a look with Clara to the question as Chase reoriented back on them.

"Yes? No?"

"We're staying at The Willard," Jason replied.

Chase raised his eyebrows at Jason's choice of accommodation.

"Love The Willard, they have the softest sheets. How are you getting there? Been drinking?"

"Get where? Everyone's been drinking," Callie asked as she appeared from the ladies' room.

"The Willard. Your buddy's staying at The Willard."

Chase's reference to Jason as her buddy bothered him, just as he intended it to.

"The Willard... Fancy," Callie replied while apologizing through her expression. "I hear it's very nice. Are you driving back in tonight?"

Clara and Jason exchanged looks again at the contradiction in Callie's and Chase's comment about The Willard.

"No," Jason answered. "We'll Uber. I'm too many drinks gone. It's five minutes out."

Callie looked to Chase who would never call an Uber, regardless of his state. The best she could hope for was for her to be sober enough to drive them home. Staying that sober had been becoming more and more of a problem lately for both of them.

"Let's go," Chase said to get away from Jason. "The car's been out front for a while."

Callie gave Jason an awkward hug before turning to drive off into the darkness with a drunk Chase.

"You should stop them," Clara stated. "He's wasted."

As Callie settled into the passenger side of the Maserati, Chase rolled past the valet, slipping him twenty dollars for taking care of his car.

"Callie!" Jason blurted as Chase was about to get in.

Jason approached the car slowly, as if only to say something to her. He did not want Chase to panic and race off. Chase remained standing as Jason neared his car. He was puzzled by the sudden need for a quick talk.

"Get out," he said, as he opened the door. "This isn't safe for you."

Callie looked to Jason as Chase started to get in the car. As he closed his door, he kept his eyes trained on Jason. The only thing that kept Chase from peeling out was the extensive damage hitting the clubhouse wall with his open passenger door would do to his car.

"Please," he added while extending his hand.

Callie unclipped her seat belt and started to exit the car. Chase followed by jumping out of his seat to run around and stop Jason from controlling his wife.

"Jason!" Clara yelled as he helped Callie onto the stairs to the building.

The cold thud that sounded as Chase's body slammed back against his car could be heard into the empty ballroom. As he slid down to a seated position on the ground, Mark stood over him to see if he needed any additional finishing off.

"You OK, buddy?" he asked as Chase moaned.

Callie looked back with little concern that her husband was possibly hurt. Clara and Jen escorted her back into the clubhouse to avoid seeing any additional measures needed to control Chase. Mark helped Chase to his feet when it was clear that the excitement was over.

After the valet returned Chase's damaged Maserati to the parking lot, Callie called for an Uber to take Chase home. He reluctantly agreed to leave without her when Callie said Sandy had invited her to stay with her and Tom. She added it was also to put her there to help set up the brunch in the morning.

Mark had his own Uber to ride back to the hotel nearby that he and Jen had chosen over bunking at Sandy's. As everyone separated into the night to their accommodations, Clara was happy to settle in her UberXL with Jason for their ride back to The Willard in comfort.

9

Sandy had already committed their guest room to her mom and dad. The best she could offer Callie was Maddie's room, which was a wreck from the wedding weekend craziness. Together they cleared the bed and changed the sheets to give Callie a comfortable and clean place to sleep. Since they were about the same size, Sandy also lent Callie pajamas to change into something more comfortable that she could wear around the house.

Callie was grateful for Sandy's help but deeply embarrassed by the events that happened at Maddie's wedding. She knew Chase was drunk. But Jason had no right to save her from her decision to let him drive them home. Mark's assault on Chase, as he tried to intervene on Jason's commandeering everything, was also inexcusable. After she finished helping Sandy put some last touches out for the out-of-towner goodbye brunch, Callie excused herself to bed.

Are you OK?

The text was waiting for her when she activated her phone. It was twenty minutes old. And it was from Jason.

Fine. You dont have to be my hero anymore. I can handle Chase

The phone sat silent for a moment before the spiral began spinning again.

I know you can. Youre a tough cookie.

The coy response irritated Callie. It was the first time since slapping Jason at his cottage that she wanted to strike him again.

Dont try to be funny. Its not your place.

Callie's reply worried Jason. Regardless of their past, pulling her out of a car with an irritated, drunk driver was the right thing to do. He thought about what he could say to cool her down. He knew she would be at Sandy's brunch in the morning.

I would have pulled anyone out of that car. Our history had nothing to do with it.

The response was not what she either wanted or expected. The chance for that ended in July when he was there for her saddest moment, and she sent him away. Callie turned her phone off as she thought about the events of the evening that led up to the final confrontation at the car. She was not careful to hide her feelings in front of Chase. He caught her with Jason leaving a side meeting room after her breakdown. And she did not act to control his alcohol intake. Callie felt responsible for what happened at the car.

Are you home?

She texted to Chase, unsure if he would still be awake to reply.

Yes

Appeared quickly as she thought about what to say next.

Are you OK? Are you hurt?

Callie knew she had to ask if he was hurt by the body slam.

I'm fine. I'm going to bed.

The bitter tone in his reply was concerning. Chase had a pattern of not calling and not responding to texts in a timely manner. But his tone was always warm and soothing. It never occurred to Callie that his tactics with her may just have been the same schmoozy charm he used on the campaign trail to cultivate endorsements and large donations. Callie waited before replying, then decided to close the conversation for the night.

Goodnight Chase

Callie waited to see the spiral start spinning on her phone to show he wanted to keep texting. After a minute of waiting, she turned her screen off and started to prepare for bed with the travel toothbrush and supplies Sandy provided.

# # #

Clara had changed into one of Jason's college t-shirts to find comfort in their room overlooking the Washington Mall. She found Jason engaged with his phone.

"What's so interesting?" she asked, frustrated that his mind was on his phone and not getting ready to snuggle with her.

"Nothing."

"Is Callie OK?"

Jason turned his phone off and turned to Clara. His look asked why she thought he was either conversing or texting with Callie. The excitement she left the bathroom with started to fade with being right.

"I was just concerned with everything that happened, that she was safe."

Jason's look of concession was enough to soothe Clara's concern. His caring nature was what she loved most about him. As she sat next to him, she rubbed his back to loosen him up to where they could get back to enjoying their night and setting.

"You're tense," she observed as she kissed his neck.

"I was feeling great when we were leaving. I just wanted to pound that asshole. Wasn't it strange that he commented on the sheets at the hotel while Callie's never stayed here?"

"Jason," Clara replied as she pressed her body against his and continued to kiss his neck, "let it go. He's a liar. He was trying to 'up' you. Who knows? Who cares?"

Jason did not hear a word Clara said as he sat thinking through Chase's exact words.

"Damn it! Jason," Clara bellowed as she pushed him away. "I'm sitting here, next to you, in just your t-shirt, kissing your neck, and you're not here."

Jason stopped to study Clara's attire. He smiled as he touched her knee. It was her sensitive spot that would always make her jump. Whether Clara was in the mood for that level of play or not remained undetermined when he squeezed his hand. As expected, she jumped with a yelp to finish and a hand slap. As she stood there with a smile on her face, Jason stood to show he was back with her, to be with her.

"If you don't mind, I'm going to take a shower first."

Clara's shoulders and jaw dropped as Jason walked away. As he disrobed, he dropped each piece of clothing like a bread crumb. Clara stood and waited as she watched him work through his routine to pull her into the shower with him. She listened as the water turned on and as he rattled items, trying to sound busy.

"Seriously?" he asked as he poked his head around the door.

"I don't want to get wet," Clara answered as she lay back on the bed. "I think I'll just rest while you shower… go ahead."

Clara waved her arms high, then stretched as she reclined onto the bed. She smiled as she heard the water stop, knowing she had won. She closed her eyes, waiting for the affection she was seeking. His presence above her was sensed before the touch of his lips on hers. Clara's back arched to the pleasure of him being completely with her. She threw her arms over his bare shoulders to pull him onto her.

10

As the Uber drove through the country club parking to pick up the Volvo, Jason noticed that his Volvo was one of many cars left overnight after the wedding. What he thought was a novel idea was shared by several other guests.

Chase's Maserati was parked in one of the wider slots reserved for more exotic cars. The placement was after the fact as Jason noticed the body-size dent behind the passenger door. Mark's crushing block of Chase into his car was reminiscent of his all-state football play in high school. Jason wondered if Mark's motivation to help was to protect his best friend or to relive his glory days after too much bourbon.

Jason loaded their bags into the Volvo as Clara settled into the passenger seat. She keyed Sandy's address into the Google maps on her phone. Sandy and Tom lived five miles from the country club. The GPS estimated the drive to take about ten minutes.

As Jason climbed into the driver's seat, he started playing with the seat adjustments.

"You drove the car here from Ashville," Clara said as he remained uncomfortable with the seat's position.

"The valet must have changed the settings," he replied.

"Then push the reset button. You're driver number one."

Jason looked to Clara as his finger pushed the driver seat preset button. The seat moved slightly back to where it originally was before he started playing with it. Clara smiled as she knew she was right.

"That's much better." He smiled, hopeful she would say nothing about being right.

# # #

As they turned from the four-lane road that connected the country club lane to Sandy's neighborhood, Jason felt a familiarity with the perfect properties they were passing. Each home was large with a sprawling lawn, gardens, and long driveway. Jason smiled when he realized why the neighborhood looked familiar. He remembered Callie's home on his computer when he Google-mapped her address years ago.

Sandy's home was a brick, English Tudor style. The wood beams and white stucco siding was properly portioned to the dark brick on all the exterior walls of the house. A ten-foot-wide surface of Belgian walk transitioned the road to the semicircle governor's driveway that delivered guests to the front door. As Jason parked behind other early arrivals near the end of the exit side of the driveway, he took hold of Clara's arm as she unbuckled her seatbelt.

"In case I don't later say it, thank you for putting up with everything this weekend."

Clara smiled, knowing the effort Jason made to make his friend's wedding weekend special for her. The special room at The Willard, passing on the rehearsal dinner for a couple's dinner in the city, and his out-of-character embellishments on the dance floor when Clara caught the bouquet and he grabbed the garter.

"Outside of the insanity of the night's end," she started, "and your predisposition to stress and protect your ONE, the weekend has been really special. Thank you for having the courage to bring me."

Jason started to speak as Clara talked about Callie. But Clara put her finger on his lips to stop him. The comment was as much a joke as it was a declaration that Clara knew that Callie still had a pull on him. His predisposition to take care of her was apparent each time she saw him with her. She knew that 'married' Callie would remain one of his demons to deal with. Her hope was that Callie stayed married and in Great Falls. Now was her time to take Callie's spot in his heart.

The walkway to the large, brownish-yellow oak door was Pennsylvania bluestone. Jason recognized the material and admired the workmanship. His home in Cleveland had the same front walk. It was installed by a team of old Italian craftsmen. They spoke Italian to each other as they worked. They called themselves the over-the-hill gang.

The doorbell chimes sounded soon after he pushed the button embedded in the limestone trim that encased the doorway. The house was consistent with the party that they threw to celebrate Maddie's wedding. Sandy and Tom were living a splendid life in their Washington, DC suburb.

Clara gasped as the front door opened. Her first thought was to wonder why it was so impossible to shake the woman that Jason could not get out of his head and heart. Callie smiled when she saw them but looked tired. She was dressed in casual clothes that said she either went home to change or Sandy lent her clothes for the party.

"Hey, you guys," she said as Clara led Jason into the front hallway.

The room was consistent with the outside; its ceiling sat two stories above the floor. An oak staircase started upward on the left wall, then turned to finish up to the second floor on the back wall. A wrought-iron railing lined the interior track of its climb. The front hall was furnished with a large oak table that matched the wood on the walls.

"How are you feeling this morning?" Jason asked as he gave Callie a hug followed by a kiss on the cheek.

Clara saw Callie's body relax as she wrapped her arms around him. She began to count as their embrace lasted longer than she thought was needed.

"I'm good," Callie answered. "Have a bit of a headache though."

"A little hangover is never a bad thing," Jason joked.

"Hangover, humiliation, dehydration, it's fine."

Callie looked away as she finished her thought. As she talked, Clara looked again at her clothes. Their fit appeared looser and not consistent with the fit of the clothing Clara remembered when they first met at Fox Farm. She looked to Jason to offer her support. His small return smile thanked her for her permission.

After Jason and Callie separated, Callie hugged Clara to welcome her too. Their embrace was ceremonial, absent of all warmth.

"Hey, everyone!" Sandy exclaimed as she entered the room. "I'm glad you're here. I've got a bunch of food. Champagne, mimosas."

Sandy's face was electric and brought light back into Callie's.

"Let me show you around," Sandy finished. "Tom will be excited to see you."

As they progressed through the house, each room continued the English theme of its exterior and front hall. Sandy decorated with a heavy wood design that Jason appreciated. Its masculine quality was similar to how he decorated the beach cottage and the cabin furnishings Clara deployed at Fox Farm. The feel of the home was like stepping back in time until they entered the kitchen with adjoining family room. The doorway separating the two rooms was where the old-world appointments transitioned to the twenty-first century.

Clara studied the beautiful grains in the ocean of granite countertops that covered the dark wood cabinets and the large center island. Sandy's six-burner Wolfe stove would fit perfectly in the main house kitchen, just like Callie's black Range Rover would do as the Farm's signature vehicle.

Jason waved to Tom, who was busy talking with his daughter's new mother- and father-in-law. The oversized family room hosted leather furniture similar to his at the cottage, complemented by the same knotty, wide plank pine floor found throughout the first floor covered by dark oriental rugs. On the wall, between two sets of shelves that bordered the fireplace, was an eighty-five-inch flat screen TV. Jason thought the room size, along with the TV size, would put him right into any game he wanted to watch.

"This is fantastic," Jason said as he turned to Sandy.

Clara was still admiring the kitchen as she walked to join them.

"This gives me some ideas for the main house," she joked as she rejoined the group.

Jason's eyes lifted at the suggestion. Clara seemed to like the amenities and toys of Northern Virginia and the upper crust.

The balance of the walk through included the backyard that extended over fifty yards back to the property line bordered by evergreens. Callie disappeared back into the house to tend to the food as Sandy continued the tour. Clara went with her to find the restroom and to get some drinks.

"I had no idea you lived like this," Jason said as he put his arm around Sandy. "I should have married you."

"Then you'd be living in an apartment somewhere," she laughed. "Tom makes the money in his tech business."

"Ahhhhh, government contractor... Belt... way... bandit," Jason joked.

"That's all I can tell you." She laughed.

"Understood." Jason laughed. "It explains Mark's tour in Europe. CIA? Is this secret government work a family thing?"

"You know I can't tell you," Sandy joked. "And it's only because neither of them tell me."

Jason smiled at her admission as he continued to survey the yard. Their back patio was the same Pennsylvania bluestone as the front walk. By his eye, it measured fifteen by twenty feet.

"If you like this," Sandy whispered, "you should see Callie's home."

"Why?"

"It's the showcase of the neighborhood," Sandy answered.

"This house, YOUR HOUSE... is a freaking showcase home," Jason replied.

"No, this is ordinary."

Jason noticed Sandy's not-so-subtle inference to Callie's life in Great Falls.

"Well, from what I hear, her husband makes a ton of dough," Jason added to fill the void.

"Yeah?" Sandy answered. "From WHOMMMM?"

Sandy's sarcasm was a shielded message. Jason's expression of happy interest in her yard dropped to concern.

"Just tell me what you're trying to say."

Sandy pulled Jason to the corner of the patio, away from the other brunch guests. She pretended to be pointing to some plants as she whispered.

"Tom thinks they're living on a financial bubble," Sandy whispered. "Chase makes a good living. But their lifestyle is way above ours, which, believe me, is really expensive. Chase is a spender. And Callie just lets him go. Tom thinks there's no way they can afford everything they have and show."

"Jesus..." Jason pondered. "Well, she's got money, and he looks like he's from an old money, preppy, overprivileged douchebag background."

He laughed as he finished his insult.

"Look, she doesn't think we think anything like this. So, you can't ask her about anything."

"It explains a lot," Jason thought out loud. "Wow."

Jason shook his head and took a deep breath to calm as he looked off into the sky. Sandy stayed silent as she watched the gears turn in his head.

"What's so interesting?" Clara asked, returning with three flutes of mimosa.

She handed one to both Sandy and Jason as their faces turned from concern to content. Clara raised her glass to keep pushing the mood to higher ground.

"To the mother of the bride, our host, and to a really fun weekend I'll never forget."

"Wait!" Sandy asked before their flutes clinked. "And... to the best, most memorable, and *fucking* funniest bouquet garter routine I've ever witnessed. You two added to the show and, in MY very humble opinion, are made for each other."

Jason winked at Clara as their three glasses came together. Smiles turned to laughter as each took a drink while thinking back over Clara's bouquet catch and Jason's presentation of the garter. None of the three noticed Callie standing behind them who heard Sandy's toast and sentiment. Callie turned to return to the kitchen before being seen and embarrassed again.

#

Callie checked her phone for messages. She left it on the counter to charge and be available in case Chase wanted to reach out to her. As her phone opened, no new messages populated the screen.

Are you coming over?

Callie pushed Send, not knowing if Chase would answer. Her concern was that he was still sleeping off the night before. The swirl began showing he was typing a reply.

No

Callie looked at his short answer, more angered that it was short than curt.

Come over. Show your face. Support our friends.

Callie waited, then watched the swirl roll again.

Are they there?

Callie closed her eyes to process Chase's fear of Jason and Mark. The thought of why he was avoiding them should have been clear.

Just Jason.

The swirl started to turn again.

Enjoy your boyfriend.

Fuck, Callie thought to herself. She could not have her husband afraid of her former fiancé. The drunken assault the night before was a misunderstanding.

btw, I got a call from the club prez this AM. Your boyfriend and his bestie are banished from the club

The news brought a smile to Callie's face. In hindsight, she should have expected the call and the action. Banishing Mark and Jason would mean nothing to them while sending a message to all members to keep their guests under control. Worse things had happened involving members, and their kids, that only resulted in a large bill to fix what they broke. The rumors were often more painful.

Callie knew that both Mark and Jason would find their banishment funny. As she envisioned the congratulatory high five they would give each other, Mark and Jen entered the kitchen from the living room. Not wanting to talk to him, Callie waved as she put her phone to her ear. She pointed outside to direct 'banished one' to 'banished two' who was on the back patio with Sandy.

Sandy noticed Mark through the French doors as he made his way to the patio. Her happy face dropped to show her anger as he and Jen walked to them.

"Good," she said. "Now that you're both here, I've got some news."

Jason shared a glance with Mark who shook his head.

"As of today..." Sandy started, "because of last night... neither of you are to set foot on Great Fall's Country Club property ever again."

Mark smiled as he looked at Jason.

"There IS a big dent in his car," Jason mumbled as he started to laugh.

"So, so, worth it," Mark proclaimed as he raised his hand to high five his mate.

"What!?" Sandy reacted. "This is my club! The rumors of a fight at Maddie's wedding that included Chase are going to be brutal on us... and on Callie."

Mark's celebration ended with Sandy's proclamation.

"I'm sorry, sis," he apologized. "How can I make this better for you?"

Sandy looked at Mark, then exhaled to release her anger. A smile appeared on her face as she looked at the two guys who always looked out for her as a child. Sandy's change relit smiles in Mark and Jason as they began to laugh again. Clara, who had remained silent through Sandy's news and condemnation, shared an awkward smile with Jen, who also knew it was best just to let Sandy deal with it.

"How would you like to tour the house?" Jen offered to Clara. "I think we should let the boys enjoy their moment. Sandy, we can help inside too."

"Oh my God." Sandy laughed. "I forgot about the rest of the party. Are people inside?"

Jen nodded yes as Sandy darted back to the house. Callie was in the kitchen keeping busy with the caterer. She was happy to see Sandy appear until she saw Jen and Clara close behind. Without direction, each woman settled in to help place the food and to inform guests that brunch was served.

11

"I can't believe we've been banished from the country club." Mark laughed as he shook his head. "I gotta tell you though, it felt good to line him up and level him."

Mark dipped his shoulder as he recalled the two-step run he took to intercept and obliterate Chase.

"It's no big deal." Jason laughed. "He's got at least ten grand in damage on his car."

Mark smiled as he moved his contact shoulder with a grimace before reaching into his pocket.

"It's morning," Jason stated as Mark pulled out a cigar case.

"Come on," Mark replied. "We'll have to go to the other end of the yard. Sandy hates the smell."

Jason shook his head as he exhaled toward his friend.

"Her and everyone else."

"OK then," Mark replied as he started walking onto the grass. "I'll be back in a few."

Jason watched as his best friend from childhood walked halfway across the yard before launching a big plume of white smoke. The trail followed him to the end of the yard, then dissipated into the air.

"Jason."

The voice was soft. It was also the one he had ached to hear for nearly thirty years. And, as he turned to see her, he noticed a defeated look on her face.

"What's wrong, Callie. If it's about the banishment... I..."

"No." She smiled. "It's not about that. Although it will become legend."

Jason knew the ramifications that were coming from Mark's assault on Chase. He appreciated the fact that Callie was not mad. He was also enjoying the fact that Chase was nowhere to be seen.

"I just wanted to tell you I'm sorry," she said.

"Callie, we've had this conversation," he answered. "Whatever you decided was best for you, was best for me. I've accepted that."

Callie showed a tormented smile as Jason finished. She thought it was ironic that when they first reconnected, his goal was to find and apologize to her for their engagement breaking. During her mother's hospital stay, he visited her dad's grave to apologize to him. And, before he left her mother's funeral, after learning she was choosing Chase over him, he turned to drive back into the cemetery, for what she believed was to apologize to her mother before leaving for good. Now, it was her turn.

"All we do is hurt and apologize to each other," she said as she ran her hand through her hair.

"People do what they do best," he joked to ease her stress.

"What's wrong with us? What's wrong with me?"

Jason moved toward Callie to touch her shoulder. Her head was down as she stared at the Pennsylvania bluestone below her. Her mind was blank, having no thoughts or answers to her questions.

"I'm so fucked," she whispered. "God put you in my life at its darkest moment, and I send you away to fall in love."

Jason pulled Callie close as she confessed. He could not deny the truth in her statement.

"I'm married to a pompous asshole," she added as she broke into a light, nervous laughter.

Jason squeezed tighter at she turned to him.

"My mother's estate is being finalized soon," Callie said in a low voice.

"That's a difficult time, particularly with the finality it has," Jason recalled.

"It sucks. And it's a lot of money I have to deal with."

Jason could hear the message Callie was sending. Sandy's observation was likely right in her assessment of Callie and Chase's finances. He ran the pros and cons of talking honestly with her.

"Cal, I don't know your situation and don't want to know," Jason started. "But, if you're worried about anything, keep everything in your name and in separate brokerage accounts… just like we talked, no, FOUGHT about when we were engaged. That ensures that whatever happens, you are financially secure."

"He just—"

Jason touched his fingers to her lips to stop her confession. He exhaled heavily while working to put together the words she needed to hear. When they did not come, he pulled his fingers away to let her finish.

"My dad's will listed Chase and me to inherit what he left me. He firmly believed that was the only way to do it."

Jason knew what she was going to say next. Callie's inheritance from her mother was larger than the first and that Chase would be taking half.

"Fortunately, my mom said that she never agreed with that philosophy and cut all the spouses out of her will after he died."

"Then you'll be fine," Jason replied. "Your mom was a smart cookie."

Callie looked to him, showing appreciation for his humor. Her face lit recalling her mother's matter-of-fact position on who was to inherit her estate. With all of their discussions on faith and life commitments, Callie's mother understood that it took two to make a marriage successful. Callie's split from Chase just before her mother died confirmed to both of them that her mother was right again.

"She loved you," Callie said as she wrapped her arms around him. "I still do too."

Jason completed her embrace by wrapping his arms around her. As their embrace lingered, Jason knew they had to separate. Clara's time away was long enough that she should be circling back. Mark was still standing at the end of the yard finishing his cigar. He had a few more moments with Callie before their privacy would end.

"I've got to make it work," Callie declared.

"No, Cal, you don't," Jason answered. "You only have to work through things to make you happy."

"Then I'll be alone."

Jason did not know if Callie's comment was rhetorical or fishing for his availability. He could not push her deeper by saying he was with Clara now. Instead, he pulled her to him again to secure her with a hug.

"You'll be fine," he answered.

"How will I be fine when my kids don't even want to come home?" she questioned. "I'm alone."

Jason remembered the same pain when his marriage was failing. His daughters found every reason not to be home and communicate. They would appear for holidays and birthdays, then have reasons to return to work or school. Like him, Callie still had two kids in college that, until this year, were home for summers. Her son, Will, had accepted an internship in New York City, expecting to only spend the first and last week of summer in Great Falls. Lizzie, her daughter, asked for permission to go to the Outer Banks for two weeks after school ended. Unknown to Callie, she was going with hope to find work and to stay with friends. Lizzie's housemate at school had a job in place and was staying in her parents' cottage a row back from the water. Lizzie knew that Callie would be crushed by her not wanting to be home for the summer. So, her decision was to ask when she could say she found a job and a safe place to live.

Jason reached to rub her back as he searched for a solution to pull Callie out of crisis. She needed him to be there for her. The torture of her long journey was rising again.

# # #

Clara arrived with a plate of food for both of them. Callie used her need to build her plate as an excuse to return to the house. She declined Jason's offer to take hers based on the amount of food Clara had placed on it. The mushrooms in the souffle was an added opportunity to say no.

"That looked intense," Clara said as they sat next to each other on a cushioned teak loveseat. "Fallout from last night's run-in?"

Jason was chewing as he pondered Clara's question. He lifted his eyebrows as she waited for him to finish.

"It's a mess," he answered. "That poor girl is being put through the ringer… and she knows it."

Jason's sympathy was obvious. It ran deeper than a friend's concern for the well-being of another. His mental wheels were spinning as he continued to eat his breakfast. Clara knew that if she asked him in an hour what he ate, he would not be able to answer.

"All right," Mark said as he and Jen arrived with their plates.

With only two chairs on the opposite end of the loveseat, Mark sat on the far end closest to Jason while Jen settled next to Clara. The wash of stale cigar smoke still lingered and reached Jason's nose as he continued to eat his meal.

"So, how's your new adventure?" Mark asked. "Living at the beach? How's that?"

Jason gave a quick look to Clara, then to Jen as he thought about his reply.

"It's great," he answered. "But... it wasn't enough. I had to get busy again."

Mark smiled when he saw Clara pull back slightly. She was not sure if Jason's explanation of how he found Fox Farm would include her backstory and his white knight save of her future and business. Mark's disposition and brutal sense of humor also offered the potential for an off-color remark about Jason dipping his pen into the company ink. Clara positioned her left hand to squeeze Jason's arm if his explanation began to run too deep.

"The cabin business is very cool and has potential," Jason added as Mark's eyes shifted from him to Clara and back. "We have a movie production company coming to scout it for an upcoming rom-com set in a setting like ours."

"A twenty-first century *Dirty Dancing*?" Mark observed.

"Maybe." Jason laughed. "I don't know. We're dealing with their scout now."

Mark looked at Clara as she leaned forward again. She was the new face that he was anxious to learn more about.

"So, Clara. How did you and this old man find each other?"

Clara looked to Jason with a nervous smile. She could see in his eyes a warning to keep things simple and separate from Fox Farm. He knew Mark would joke about company ink if she mentioned she either used to own or worked there now.

"In Lake Lure," Clara replied, hoping the obscurity of the area would not be as enticing as an Asheville reference. "We met through friends. It's near Asheville."

Clara regretted the reference to Asheville. Mark continued to smile as he looked back and forth between the two.

"That's great," he remarked. "You two look good together. You certainly can entertain a crowd."

Mark's reference to the bouquet and garter exposition offered the segue both Jason and Clara wanted to move the conversation away from them.

The rest of their time together covered stories and remembrances from Jason's youth up until Mark was transferred to England twenty years ago. After that, the stories became fewer and centered on Jason and Stephanie's visit during their daughter Rachel's study abroad. Mark observed the similarities between Stephanie and Clara to prove his point that Jason definitely had a type he was attracted to. Mark did not include Callie in his jest, having thought of it but being sober enough not to say it.

"So, what's next?" Mark asked Jason as he set his plate on the matching teak table.

"I'm heading down to the coast to check on the cottage. Maya is arriving from school to work there this summer as a lifeguard. I want to see her for a few days… Clara is flying back to Ashville to check in on the Farm for me. Life just goes on, I guess."

Jason felt a squeeze on his arm and immediately regretted the alignment of Fox Farm to Clara. He could see from Mark's expression that he was putting the details together better than either Jason or Clara wanted to share.

"That's great," Mark said as he smirked, knowing exactly what was going on. "It's good that you can cover for him like that."

Clara had to work to hold her smile as she looked at his grin. And he knew it. She was also thankful he was holding back any number of comments and funnies he could make about it.

"It's nothing, really," Clara remarked. "He's got a remarkable staff there."

Mark looked to Jen as he ran through the comments he could not make.

"I'm sure he does. Anyone would be happy to work for him."

Clara felt a warm wash of heat fill her cheeks as Mark finished his comment. She knew it was meant out of respect for his best friend and out of kindness for her. The obnoxious blowhard who drank too much and smoked cigars was becoming warm and human to her. She could now see why he was Jason's best friend.

"Oh, and if you need extras, or a leading man, for the movie shoot, I'm available."

The four laughed at Mark's offer. In Clara's opinion, the leading man was sitting beside her. She squeezed his arm again to confirm he was still real.

12

Jason and Mark are leaving. You need to make an appearance and apologize to Sandy and Tom.

As the dots started moving on her screen, Callie was happy that Chase was connected to his phone and, maybe, open to showing his face for brunch.

Later

Sandy put her hand on Callie's back as she continued to study his reply on her phone screen. Callie remained in the kitchen to focus on the food presentation and delivery. Sandy moved from group to group to ensure everyone had enough food and drink, fearful of a load of leftovers to either be tossed or dinner for the next few weeks.

"Don't push him," Sandy commented as the screen went dark. "We're all friends. And the confrontation wasn't his fault."

Callie continued to look at her iPhone's black screen as Sandy spoke. Her friend was focusing on the incident while Callie's troubles were rooted in a much larger set of circumstances.

"Thanks for that," Callie replied as she turned to hug her friend. "Thanks for everything."

"Jason's gone," Callie whispered.

"I think so too," Sandy replied. "I'm so sorry."

#

Clara's flight from Dulles International Airport near Reston, Virginia, was at three o'clock. With TSA Pre-Check on a Sunday,

Jason planned to drop her off an hour earlier then start the five-hour drive to the beach. She was anxious to get back to the cabins and the lower stress of her mountain life. When they started to say their goodbyes, they noted that most of the other brunch guests had left. As the three couples stood outside the front door, Callie lingered behind to be part of the goodbyes without being the awkward center of attention.

"You must come see us in the mountains," Clara said as she hugged Mark goodbye. "I think it would suit you."

Mark smirked as he looked to Jason that he won over Clara.

"That goes for everyone, please come visit," Clara added as she hugged each of them.

Her words were genuine, and Jason was glad to hear her express her comfort and like of his childhood friends. Jason followed as he embraced both the men and their wives to close out their time together.

As they finished the run of the couples, Clara stepped to Callie who was waiting quietly in the back.

"I hope to see you again," Clara said with empathy for her situation.

Callie smiled to her honest sentiment.

"It's unlikely," she answered. "But thank you. Me too."

Callie moved first to hug Clara, to say goodbye. Under any other situation, Clara would be a friend. Both knew that. It was unfortunate that circumstances made that impossible.

Jason stepped up as Clara let go to say his goodbye.

"Anytime, for any reason, call... come," Jason implored.

Callie reached up to hug him in the manner he remembered. The cutting pain on his shoulder he missed for decades returned for its final impression. Jason kissed her on the cheek as they separated. Tears were in his eyes to be leaving. But he knew there was little he could offer to make her life whole again.

The Volvo pulled out of the driveway, then turned to drive along the front of the manicured front yard. Jason and Clara waved to his friends, who were still standing by the front door and watching. Callie stood beside Mark as she waved goodbye. His arm was around her to comfort her through Jason's departure. The group quickly fell from sight as the Volvo disappeared off into the distance.

# # #

Callie decided to walk home from Sandy's. Her house was a few streets over in the same neighborhood. As her house came into view, she looked back to the line of sight it had to Sandy's property and backyard. She knew, from looking, that what happened in Sandy's backyard was obscured by the houses that sat between their two properties.

As she walked up the driveway to the garage, she noticed Chase had retrieved his Maserati from the country club. Seeing his car next to her Range Rover showed that he was home. Anxiety began to overwhelm her sadness as she kept walking to face what was waiting inside.

Callie touched the damage on Chase's car as she passed it in the garage. She then looked at her SUV to see if he did anything to retaliate for the damage her friends created. As her hand felt the concave dent behind the door on the quarter panel, she remembered the incident and the thud his body made when it struck and pushed in the metal surface of his car.

The door to her kitchen was less than fifteen feet away when Callie stopped to think through her next steps. She expected Chase to still be mad and to verbally assault her the moment their eyes met. She had no fear of him hitting her. Despite his many faults in anger, physical assault was not one of them.

The kitchen was empty when Callie opened the door. The house was silent except for the hum of the refrigerator. Molly woke from sleeping on the window seat and joined her as she progressed from room to room. She stayed quiet, preferring to approach softly than to demand a presence through a shout-out. Callie's anxiety grew as she continued to look, and Chase was nowhere to be found.

Callie checked her phone to see if she had any messages. She knew to look was futile because it announced everything with a dedicated tone. Callie had ringtones specific to everyone. The text tone was its own and stayed silent from her last series with him. Chase was not home. He was gone.

Are you home?

Callie texted. She was afraid to get into an argument on the phone. The text noted delivered underneath her message, showing that Chase's phone had received her question. A swirl appeared under the message, then disappeared. Happy to have connected, Callie waited for Chase's reply that did not come.

When she returned to the kitchen, she found a note from Chase on the counter.

I'm heading out to South Carolina early for my trip. I'm so angry with you that I think it's best we be apart for the next two weeks. Chase.

"Fuck," Callie whispered to herself as she put the note down.

As much as she dreaded seeing him for their initial confrontation, the pain of having him gone was worse.

Callie felt an emptiness as she looked around the kitchen she loved. Chase's timeframe put his return home into early May with the end of Will's week before heading to New York. Given Will's behavior in Williamsburg before her mom died, Will was not going to be understanding if things had blown up again with his dad.

Callie was finding it hard to deal with the silence. She knew she needed to find support. She felt that Sandy, with both the excitement of the wedding and the anxiety of the assault, was exhausted. It would be unfair to lean on her now. Callie thought about calling her kids to give herself a sense of anchor. But she felt that they would ask questions she either did not want to answer or could not answer. She decided to go for a drive into the country, maybe to see her sister Patty. But sharing this pain with her again after Patty called Callie's choice of Chase over Jason foolish, was not an attractive option to find comfort. After grabbing a Diet Pepsi from the refrigerator, she grabbed her purse, wallet, and keys to go find some solace.

# # #

The drive from Dulles International Airport to the cottage took five hours. After saying goodbye to Clara at the departure curb, Jason pulled into traffic and tuned out. The drive was simple and familiar from both his days of living in the area and attending soccer tournaments with his kids throughout the region. For five hours, Jason's radio remained silent, which was not unusual.

As he crossed the last bridge onto the island, his cell phone pinged with a message. Concerned that it might be Callie, Jason had his female Australian Siri read the message as he navigated through the lanes of light traffic.

Have arrived home. Everything in good shape. I'll call later. Love you.

Jason ran some mental calculations in his head for pre-flight waiting, her flight, waiting for her luggage, and the final drive back to Fox Farm. Five hours was about right. It seemed Clara's flight went well. He instructed Aussie Siri to reply with

that's great, almost there, talk then, love you back.

Jason smiled as Siri read back his message. He could see the ocean through the gaps between the large houses as he turned onto the road that ran behind them. He rolled his windows down to exchange his air-conditioned air with the humid coolness of a North Carolina beach spring evening.

As he pulled into the driveway, he saw the familiar red Mini Cooper convertible that he had purchased for his daughter Maya between her freshman and sophomore years. Having just one year remaining in school, Maya was taking advantage of the cottage to work and play at the beach before graduating and starting a job. Maya parked in the left slot under the house beside Jason's Jeep Wrangler. Jason parked the Volvo behind the Jeep to be able to shuffle cars later to access his preferred daily beach driver.

The properties around the cottage were lit by the familiar soft, warm glow of the setting sun. It was Jason's favorite time of day, when the heat would subside and cool breezes would flow. Maya was scheduled to arrive a few days earlier. Her charge was to text him when she arrived and any problems she found. Both he and she had forgotten to contact each other due to the excitement of their weekends.

Jason walked to the rear of the cottage that faced the ocean. So far, he was pleased to see limited wear on the exterior of the house. He and Zoe made monthly runs to visit the beach, check the house, and to see Maya and his third daughter, Faith, on spring break in early March. His relationship with Clara kept him in the mountains over the winter.

The vista that opened as he stepped past the corner of his house was always like he was seeing it for the first time. Maya was sitting in his favorite spot, on the bench overlooking the sand and the surf. She did not respond to his calls as he approached. So, he decided to text her.

The time delay from send to receive was about three seconds. With her nose already in her screen, Maya did not need a ping or buzz to grab her attention. When the text appeared, she moved the screen closer to her face, smiled, then immediately stood to find him ten feet behind her. She greeted her dad with a hug, noticeably happy that he had arrived safely and that he would be taking her out to dinner.

"What's for dinner?" Jason asked as he stepped back.

"I don't know, your treat?"

Jason gave a puzzled look to her reply.

"I think you mean, your choice?"

"Yeah," she replied with a smile. "That too."

Jason smiled as Maya stood waiting for confirmation. He shook his head as he turned to head back to the cottage. Maya circled back to the bench to put on her flip-flops. He rolled his hard-shell suitcase into the living room, then slid the door shut.

"Let's take your car. I want to ride in it to make sure everything is fine."

Jason knew the suggestion would startle Maya. Although he was being honest about wanting to ride in the Mini to make sure there were no noises or rattles to worry about, he also wanted to see how Maya was caring for the car he bought her. Maya had a tendency to let her car collect debris over time. The hope was buying her a convertible where loose things blow away would curb that bad habit.

"Ok," Maya answered reluctantly. "I may have to move a few things."

"I figured," he replied as he put his arm around his youngest to walk her toward the house.

# # #

Callie returned to her house after spending five hours walking around the Capital Mall with Molly. The house was dark except for a few lights that automatically turned on when light sensors detected that the sun had set. Chase chose those automatic switches over the traditional timers that Callie knew from her childhood that would turn on and turn off at preset times. The off switch was preset for around midnight and turned off within minutes of each other instead of all at one time.

As she pulled her Range Rover into the garage, she let the engine continue to run after she put the car in park and pushed the button to close the door behind her. The overhead light lit as she heard the hum of the opener working above her. Callie thought about how easy it would be to let her car continue to run. She would fall asleep with Molly beside her to hopefully wake with her mother and father in a better place. Callie closed her eyes as she relaxed in her leather seat, listening to the hum of her engine fill the garage with carbon monoxide.

A ping from her phone pulled her from her relaxed state as a message appeared on her screen.

I made it. I'm at the beach!

In all the insanity of the day, Callie forgot that her daughter, Lizzie, was traveling from school to the beach after finals. Callie and Chase had given her permission to drive her car from school in Harrisonburg, Virginia to Kill Devil Hills as long as she had another driver with her. Lizzie agreed to the terms. But she forgot to tell them the other driver would be driving her own car, and that their trip was a small convoy of friends with their own rides.

The image of Lizzie's face that appeared in Callie's consciousness made her sit up and turn her car off. The windows of her car were still up, which prevented the car exhaust from entering the passenger cabin. Callie opened the garage door to air out the poisonous gases she allowed to gather around her.

She reached into her purse to find her phone to reply.

Awesome sweetie, thanks for texting.

Callie smiled as she thought that Lizzie's text was probably sent a few hours after she got there. She knew the pull of the ocean and being with friends would have distracted her from the practical thing of telling Mom and Dad she arrived safely.

How was the wedding?

Callie looked at the question, thinking through the weekend's events of extraordinary love seen through the bridal couple and their parents alongside the bad feelings and actions that happened with Jason, Chase, and Mark. The three most important living men in her life came together in a perfect storm of destruction she saw coming and could not make NOT happen.

It was lovely.

Callie wrote back, using exclusion to not lie to her daughter.

Dad like it?

The question should have been expected. Callie thought about how to reply that did not sound evasive. Dots appeared as Callie thought. Lizzie was writing again.

Was Mr Cartwright there?

Surprised by the question, Callie lowered her phone to her lap. Why would Lizzie put Jason at the wedding? She then thought about the links between him, her, and Cleveland that would have brought Sandy in as a friend. Callie smiled as she thought her kids were too smart to fool.

Yes. He said to tell you hello

Callie added the sentiment to put Lizzie's mind at ease that things were OK between everyone. The dots appeared under her last text.

Is dad ok?

Callie exhaled softly as she closed her eyes. Her response had to be perfect. She needed to stop the line of questioning and soften Lizzie's concern. The last sixteen months of fighting, counseling, divorce, then not divorce were brutal on her.

Mom?

The follow-up brought a smile to Callie's face. She was the one always sending texts to unanswered questions.

*Your father is fine. He left for South Carolina
for work. He'll be gone for two weeks.*

You should go. That'd be fun.

Callie thought to herself that Lizzie was right. South Carolina would be fun if he was on the coast. But this campaign's hub was based in Spartanburg in the western part of the state. And although beautiful with mountains and lakes, there would be little for her to do there while he was busy.

It would be. Hes not at the beach

Lizzie took an unusual pause before replying.

OK mom. Got to go. Dinner time.

Callie touched Lizzie's final message as she continued to sit in her car. The garage opener's overhead light had turned off as her screen provided the only illumination beyond floor lights. Callie grabbed her purse and opened her door to leave. Molly jumped at the sound and as light filled the cabin.

As she entered her empty kitchen, Callie pushed the button to close the garage door. The garage air was clear, with only a slight smell of exhaust lingering. Callie had found a new desire to live through her brief exchange with Lizzie. She was mad at herself for her selfishness to have even toyed with an attempt to end her pain for good. She started to make a mental list of things to get done tomorrow. Sandy would need help with the cleanup from the weekend and brunch. Monday was going to be the start of the rest of her life.

13

The Wolfpack red Mini Cooper convertible, with the two white racing stripes down its bonnet, nosed into a parking space at Mikey's that faced the front porch dining area. The restaurant sat in the second row of buildings from the ocean. It was a converted older home with two levels of balcony facing the ocean. A series of recently built, low-level condo buildings obstructed the dining view of the water. But in the right seat, at the right table, it was possible to see between the buildings to get a glimpse of the sand and the surf.

Mikey's was a place Jason and Maya frequented. The seafood was fresh and prepared with little fanfare. Their seafood pizza was loaded with a variety of crustaceans sautéed in garlic butter and landed on a chewy crust buttered with the same sauce. The pizza was best as a dine-in. For takeout and delivery, Jason used a closer pizzeria that was more traditional. Because of the cool air, Jason and Maya chose to sit inside near the bar.

"Your car could use a clean out," Jason mentioned as he settled into his chair.

"Yeah," Maya answered. "You know, the travel down, moving here for the summer."

"It's a three-hour drive," Jason answered, then added with Maya's usual sarcastic supply, "I know, for you maybe."

Maya's attempt to make her move to the beach as anything more than a short drive was not going to fly. He needed to convince her that messy cars lead to messy homes that lead to messy lives. Although, he was not one to talk about that.

As they waited for service, Maya sat quietly with a smirk on her face. Jason ignored it at first, but then it began to bug him.

"What?" he finally interjected.

Maya's smirk expanded to a smile as she started nodding her head.

"I've got nothing," she answered to egg him on.

"What?... Really?"

Maya knew her silence was becoming annoying and wanted to push it a little further to really get under his skin.

"Spill it. What's going on?"

Maya exhaled as she ran her fingers through her hair.

"Nothing Dad, really," Maya answered as she moved her head to push her hair behind her shoulders. "I'm not the one who had the big weekend."

Maya could not resist adding a sarcastic tone to her statement. She watched as Jason rolled his eyes in recognition that she knew where he was and who was also going to be there. His relationship with Clara, that cost Maya ten bucks in her sisters' Callie or Clara pool, meant that he either flew solo through the weekend or took Clara as his plus-one. Maya also figured that there was no way Clara would let Jason go to Washington alone even if Callie was back with her husband. Maya and her sisters talked about how they thought the entire story would make a great Netflix mini-series. And who would play whom.

"Yes, well," Jason started. "It was a lovely event..."

Maya stared to show she wanted to hear more.

"And?" she added.

"And... the entire wedding was top drawer. It was fabulous. And I hope to GOD that you and your sisters don't want something that elaborate."

Jason was trying to push her buttons to head off into a tangent conversation. Maya knew what he was doing.

"And?"

"And?" Jason added, "I saw my best friend from childhood. The couple we visited in London when Rachel studied abroad. That was really awesome."

Jason smiled to emphasize seeing Mark as his reason to go. He was again hoping to drive the conversation in that direction. Rachel spent time with Mark and Jen while in the same city. He knew Maya knew some of those stories.

"Come on, and?" Maya pushed.

"Well." He paused to think of something innocuous to bore her with. "The drive was really easy. It's amazing how I can still get around Northern Virginia without a—"

"DAD! Come on." Maya finally surrendered. "Did you take Clara? If so, was Callie there? Did it create a problem? ... Oh, and was there a fight?"

Maya laughed as she sarcastically delivered her final question. In her mind, she saw Clara and Callie going at each other over her dad. Jason continued to smile as he watched his daughter's face freeze while she watched the screen in her head. He knew exactly what she was thinking. It was a good thing for him that she did not have a way to learn how close her question was to what happened.

"I did.... She was.... I don't think so.... and they didn't fight."

Jason tried to answer each question in the order they were asked. His final answer, however, was limited to Callie and Clara and not a direct answer to what Maya asked.

"Oh," Maya answered, trying to match his list of responses to her questions. "That's good."

Jason relaxed as he became more comfortable with his answers as the truth.

"So you fought someone?" Maya asked as her eyes lit to the realization he just skirted around her final question.

Jason laughed as she focused in on him.

"No," he answered truthfully, "but there was a little scuffle between Mr. Fisher and Callie's husband that resulted in some damage to his car.... And that's all you get to know."

"Oh my God, this is rich." Maya chuckled. "What kind of damage? Was anyone hurt?"

"No," Jason replied, loving his daughter's fascination with what happened. "No one was hurt. And my guess is that the damage to the Maserati was about ten grand."

"Maserati!? Jesus." Maya laughed.

"Yes, and this goes no further," Jason added.

"I need to hear more details.... And how Clara handled all of it."

"Let me get a drink first."

Chase arrived at his Airbnb later than he expected. His flight change from Monday to Sunday was best accommodated through a direct flight to Charlotte and a rental car drive for two hours to Spartanburg. The car he rented, although premium, was barely adequate in both power and amenities. His thought during the drive was that he should have driven the Maserati. But a car like that with the damage it had would raise eyebrows both for the fees Chase was charging and how the damage happened. Its size and location on the car would be hard to explain.

As he opened the door to the apartment, he put his satchel on the dining room table then rolled his suitcase to the bedroom. The apartment was going to be his base camp for two weeks of continuous action to re-elect one of South Carolina's sitting US Senators who was struggling. Chase expected that the effort would have to include some above and below the table activity to ensure victory in November. With the spring primaries approaching, his Democratic opponent would be identified from the pool of six that were running. It was important to the Republicans maintaining control of the Senate that Chase bring home a winner. Doing that would catapult his career back to where it had been before a recent dry spell in results and work. A lull that was beginning to be too long and was starting to affect his client list and cash flow.

Chase linked his phone to his rental car's Bluetooth before he left the airport. He watched for texts from Callie to ask where he was and to see if he arrived. He thought by nine o'clock, she would have surrendered to ping him with something.

Where r u?

The question appeared on his phone screen without any accompanying noise. Chase intentionally kept his text notifications off while on tour. He kept his phone in his pocket. The vibration was all he wanted as notice for a message. He smiled as the phone's vibration on the Airbnb's table confirmed he was right to wait.

As he picked up the phone, he looked to see the message. The writing was cryptic and hurried. It was not how Callie communicated. When he read the name *Sarah Shallot* above the message, the tenseness he felt to hear from Callie released to a warm rush through his body.

In town. Came early. To see you.

Sarah Shallot grew up near Raleigh, North Carolina. She attended an all-girls liberal arts college that road-tripped often to Jason Cartwright's alma mater. The eighteen-year difference between Jason and Sarah meant they could never have met.

Want me to *come* over?

Chase smiled at the message. Sarah's career started as a low-level staffer in DC who had risen through positions in both House and Senate offices throughout the southeast. Sarah was Chase's advocate with her boss to manage his re-election campaign. The two met three years earlier when Chase was saving a house campaign in north Florida. Their affair started at that victory party and only took one short break when Chase dumped her to save his marriage after Callie's October visit to the Outer Banks.

Chase knew if Callie had not called by nine, that she would not be calling before the morning. He texted the address of the Airbnb to Sarah with a smiley face. She confirmed with a thumbs up and a heart. Their touches were over until she got there.

FYI. I arrived in Spartanburg. Have a good night.

Chase sent the text to Callie as insurance she would not call. He knew the curt messaging would anger her, while knowing he was there would eliminate her curiosity. Dots appeared to show she received his message and wanted to reply. His hope was for her to show some remorse for the assault he endured over the weekend.

Congratulations

Chase read her response twice, then laughed as he put his phone on the table. Callie was mad and, therefore, taken care of for the night. Sarah was on her way over to take care of Chase. He opened his suitcase to find his shaving kit. He wanted to have fresh breath for when Sarah arrived.

# # #

Two days at the beach had Jason relaxed. He was back into his routine that included his morning swims and coffee. The May water was cooler than he liked but far warmer than Jersey Shore water in July when he used to vacation with his ex-wife's family. Regardless, the exercise felt good to get his entire body back into motion. Mountain hikes and runs with Zoe and Clara, along with the occasional man's work around Fox Farm, was not enough to keep him in shape.

Maya started her training to lifeguard at the stations set up along the sand. Her office was going to be an elevated wood chair with only a towel to sit on for comfort. Jason suggested that she train at the NC State pool before showing up for work at the beach. He used to watch the lifeguards in Jersey train. His word to describe it was *'military.'* Maya took his suggestions and started swimming laps during her last four weeks of school. She found that the workouts also helped improve the clarity of her thinking leading into exams. She was hopeful the enhanced clarity would result in a positive impact on her spring semester final grades.

Jason was sitting in his usual spot on the bench overlooking the beach. His flippers and lifesaving bullet hung on the pegs he installed for them. The sun was on its decline behind him as he enjoyed the smells and sounds of the ocean. He was sipping on a double Roughrider and periodically reaching down to pet Zoe, who should have been next to him. He regretted not figuring out a way to take her with them to the wedding. He missed having her there at the beach.

"I quit," Maya announced from behind.

She finished her walk to him with heavy feet pounding on the deck. Her shoulders drooped from exhaustion.

"I should've gone home and guarded at one of the pools."

Jason laughed as he watched his youngest make her adjustment from the minors to the big leagues in lifesaving. Her days of using shepherd's hooks and jumping into clear, clean water to snag a child that drifted too far into the pool's deeper water were over.

"You know," she said pointing at his swimming aids, "your gear is what we use… except our flippers are made that way. Yours are homemade."

Jason listened as Maya made fun of his gear. His awareness of the shortened flippers came from watching lifeguards in Jersey fly into and through the water to swim quickly to swimmers in distress. Their short length gave nimbleness while the webbing effect and added inches gave the swimmer drive and speed through the water. Jason bought the floating bullet as a safety device for him because he swam alone in the tides. At any point, he could buoy-up on it to either take a rest or ride out a rip current. He used it several times the previous summer to fish out a few teenage swimmers that got in trouble.

"I couldn't find your professional flippers anywhere. So, I made mine." Jason smiled, thinking his were fine.

"I don't know why you do that. Why do you cheap out on yourself? You're not hurting for money."

Jason looked at his daughter, who spent every cent she made along with the allowance and credit card he provided her. He wondered if he was doing her any favors. But he also knew she was practical in what she bought. She was a spender that bought quality over flash. That was one quality he was proud that he and his ex-wife embedded in all their children. They were privileged but not spoiled.

"What do you say we go get some red meat tonight?" Jason asked, looking for a change from their seafood and pizza diet from the past two nights.

He knew Maya would benefit from some additional iron in her bloodstream. A perfect burger or steak sounded great. Jason had already called the reservation into The Shack, where he took Callie on her first night with him. The crowds would still be light on a midweek, early May night. But he wanted to be sure his table was waiting.

Maya nodded to agree, then headed to the shower. Their seven-thirty reservation was going to work well for her to clean up, go out, then hit the hay to get a good night's sleep to do it all over again in the morning.

14

"I heard there was a ruckus at the Fisher-Worth wedding on Saturday." Patty smiled as Callie sat watching her prepare dinner.

Her expression remained calm except for the appearance of a slight smile on the right side of her face. She knew her older sister would hear about what happened. Given the massive amount of guests, the grapevine reached everywhere.

Callie waited a few days to work through her issues privately before connecting with anyone. Her mother was her usual go-to. But she was now gone. Her next best touchstone was always Patty. Of her two sisters, Patty was the most like Callie. She also lived less than twenty-five minutes away.

Over the days since the wedding, Patty heard several different versions of the same stories. Regardless of which version was true, the common thread was that Callie and Chase were in the middle of it. She was waiting for Callie's call. And when it did not come within a few days, Patty called Callie.

Her plan was to invite Callie to help make dinner. Her early arrival would give them time to talk before her husband Brian and two sons came home. And, even though the time before her family would be home was short, Patty knew it would be good for Callie to get a solid opportunity to vent before spending time with family who loved her.

"I knew that night was going to be trouble," Callie stated, showing her frustration. "I had to be there for Sandy. Jason was there for Mark. Chase NEVER would have let me go solo. It was the perfect storm coming together. I'm actually surprised it took that long to develop."

Callie thought back over the day's events. There was no doubt to her that Chase walked into the church with a chip on his shoulder to make the day and evening miserable for Jason. She shook her head with a smile as she thought about the bouquet toss.

"What?" Patty asked. "Tell me!"

Callie took a moment to form her thoughts. She wanted to give the story its true justice. The entire event could not have been choreographed better. She knew Chase was right. If Clara had been her, she would not have handled Clara's handling of the bouquet toss debacle as elegantly. She was also surprised, and impressed, with Jason's rise to the occasion to make the entire, unimportant aspect of the reception memorable.

"It was quite something," Callie said, smiling.

Patty looked to notice Callie smiling. She stopped chopping, then put her knife down. The stories that flowed from the wedding were more than just the fight at the end. The bouquet toss with two fifty-somethings performing the catch and always embarrassing garter ceremony was what was also lighting up the community grapevine. Who the two were did not get included in the details.

"I heard about that too." Patty laughed, sorry to have missed it.

"Yeah, Jason's date, Clara, was egged on by Jason and Mark to participate. She did what I would have done. You know, stand at the back to fake it."

Patty's took a taste of wine as Callie built her story.

"I didn't know that's who it was... or that he brought a date!" Patty declared.

"Yep, it gets better," Callie answered. "Maddie launches this high throw that all the girls go for then pop it back up like a volleyball to the back of the group, and as the group shifted to chase it, they knocked Clara on her ass and the bouquet falls right into her lap."

Patty bent over the kitchen island, frozen in surprise. Her mouth hung open as her eyes urged Callie to keep going.

"I would have been mortified," Callie admitted. "But she just jumped up, and I mean JUMPED UP to her feet and pointed the bouquet right at Jason. She was obviously embarrassed. But she made the most of it by staking her claim on him by pointing those fucking flowers right at him."

Callie's voice dropped with her final comment. Patty knew there had to be more to it.

"And?"

Callie responded with a closed-mouth laugh that exhausted through her nose. She changed position on her stool as she constructed that side of the story in a fitting manner.

"Well, as a tit for tat for his date, Jason had to do the garter catch. Being six foot four, he towered over most of the single guys who had absolutely no interest in catching the garter."

Patty smiled at the vision. "They never do. Particularly to put it on a fifty-year-old woman."

"I know, right," Callie replied before taking a sip of wine. "So, Ramon, the groom, shoots the garter high above their heads and it drops into Jason's hand as if he was trying to deliver it to him. Jason couldn't drop it."

"Oh my God." Patty laughed while envisioning the unfolding of what was to come. "If I had been his date, I would have killed him if he didn't catch it."

"Well, and God bless her, Clara walks out with total attitude, spins, and sits on the chair they had for her while he stood off to the side. He then did this three step, pause, and slide to a kneel thing that was... perfect."

Callie stopped as she thought about the action and the right word to use. It was the perfect finish to the most awkward, and fun, start to a bouquet toss she had ever seen.

"Then what?" Patty asked to pull Callie back from her thoughts.

"That was it," she answered. "He did the slow garter thing up her leg. But as sexy as they played that to be, everything before it was better. He also made sure she got applause at the end. It was so sweet... and so... him."

Patty watched Callie withdraw into her head. The laughter that came with the description evaporated to sorrow because of who the couple was, and how well they acted together. Patty could hear from Callie's description of Jason and Clara together that she had lost him.

"So what happened at the end of the night?"

The question pressed on Callie's shoulders as she thought through how to explain that event. To be truthful would require framing Chase as an asshole and a drunk. It would also have celebrated Jason as her hero. Patty did not support Callie taking Chase back when their mother died ten months earlier. She went as far as to tell her that.

Although Jason had held the top position on the family's shit list for decades, his return, and how he did it, changed how Callie's sisters and mother felt about him. Chase's admission, during counseling, of his numerous affairs, and Callie's pursuit to divorce him, catapulted him over Jason to number one. In Patty's mind, Chase was still bad news. But she supported her sister's choice to give him another chance and hoped for the best.

Patty waited for Callie to compile her thoughts, knowing she wanted to answer the question. She also knew that Callie was framing everything to represent the truth, without bashing her husband in the process.

"It was a misunderstanding," Callie started. "Through the evening Chase made some rude comments around, and to, Jason. I think the bouquet thing made him more jealous. Then he caught me talking with Jason and made a comment about us having a quickie, before threatening him. That's when he stepped in to defend me. JASON was defending ME against my husband."

The backstory Callie was providing painted a much different picture than what was being circulated through the rumor mill. Patty's expression went flat as she waited for the rest of Callie's version.

"I had no idea," Patty said to give her more time.

Callie's expression showed she was reconstructing a painful series of events in her head. Patty reached to touch her hand to give her support.

"Well, fast forward to leaving," Callie blurted to get the story going again. "I'm in the restroom. Chase's car is out front. He's frantic because he wants to go."

Callie touched a napkin to her eye as she continued.

"Jason, Mark, Clara, and Jen all arrive at the door to head home before I come out. I guess Chase asked where he was staying in order to make some asshole comment about it—"

"Where was that?" Patty interjected, wanting more detail.

"The Willard. He was staying at The Willard."

Patty's head tilted as her expression changed. She seemed both surprised and impressed by Jason's choice.

"That's pretty far from the golf club. Especially after drinking."

Callie listened as Patty set her scene for her. Her face trembled as she struggled to keep from crying.

"He drove out in his car then Uber'd home in a big GMC, something like my old Suburban."

Patty began tabulating costs in her head of the room cost and an Uber ride thirty minutes to the city then back to pick up his car.

"That's an expensive weekend."

"No kidding," Callie answered. "Likely to thank Clara for putting up with having me around."

Patty smiled to sympathize with her younger sister. She then thought about her husband and two teenage boys. Patty was building a renewed appreciation for how lucky she was that she found one of the few beltway bandits that could make a big living without it going to his head. She looked at the clock to check the time. Her family was due to arrive in minutes, and she wanted Callie to finish before she could not speak in front of them.

"So, what happened?"

"Well, Chase was drunk. Which makes Jason's Uber thing so much more 'right,'" she added. "I got into the car as Chase stumbled around to get into the driver side. Before he was in, Jason opened the door and told me to get out. He knew Chase was drunk... Jen told Sandy that Clara actually was the one that got him to act."

"So, in comes Mr. White Knight again," Patty replied, trying to add humor.

"So, I'm getting out, and Chase comes flying around the car to confront him."

"And Jason slugs him?" Patty questioned. "I heard there was a big dent in his car?"

"No." Callie chuckled. "Mark, Sandy's older brother, and Jason's best friend from home, drills him like a football player into the side of the car. Mark's like six foot five. I thought Chase was dead from the sound it made. Maybe better if he had been."

Callie held back a smile as she finished her comment. She did not mean it. But, in the same light, there was some honesty in it.

"You said it, not me." Patty laughed.

"After that, I didn't see him. His car is really damaged. He got himself an Uber. And I stayed at Sandy's."

Callie finished the story to include her text exchanges with Chase, and Chase's unexpected early departure to his two-week assignment in South Carolina. Patty noticed that Callie's emotions were calming through the balance of her story. And that her emotions were only tied to the parts that included Jason. Patty heard the garage door opener sound as Callie was finishing her story. They had less than two minutes to wrap up things.

"I think that is the craziest series of events I've ever heard," Patty observed. "What do you want Chase to do now that he just... ran?"

"I don't know," Callie replied. "We're married.... Until death do us part, right?"

"Well, if it comes to that."

Patty sympathized with Callie as she picked up her chopping knife. She then smiled as she walked around the island to give her baby sister a long, supporting hug.

"It will be OK. I promise."

#

Chase stepped to the side of the room to check his phone. He was curious to see if Callie had sent him anything during the day. A text would have vibrated. An email to his personal Gmail would just be sitting there waiting. He was growing concerned that she had not attempted to make contact in three days. When he checked her location through his find my phone app that he promised Callie he would take her phone off, he noticed she was in Leesburg, Virginia visiting her older sister Patty.

Chase expected to find Callie at Patty's days earlier than he did. He knew Patty was now Callie's go-to when she needed help. Patty wanted Chase gone when he and Callie were in the middle of their first divorce proceedings. Callie's need for her sister changed dramatically when her mother died. It was a change that concerned him.

"Hey," Sarah said as she pulled him into a neighboring room.

A wash of her perfume filled the air around him as she pushed her long blonde hair behind her ear.

"Since we have the weekend, I want to do something really cool. Maybe we can rent a boat on Lake Hartwell near Clemson or run up into the mountains."

Sarah's excitement aroused him. She did a small dance with her thin, thirty-nine-year-old body. Her excitement to be with him was what he loved most. Chase smiled as he bumped into her before heading back to finish his work.

"Bad idea?" she asked.

"No. Great idea," he answered with a reassuring smile. "But I won't be able to leave here until at least seven o'clock on Friday. Wherever we choose, it has to be somewhere drivable. A boat sounds great. But check the weather."

"I'll surprise you," Sarah answered. "I am sooo excited."

Chase nodded as Sarah pranced off. The bounce in her step inflated his ego that a beautiful blonde thirty-nine-year-old wanted him. He checked his phone again for messages from Callie and to keep tabs on her whereabouts. His app still had her blue dot sitting in Patty's house.

We need to talk.

The text appeared as Patty's family entered from the garage. Callie's phone was on the counter, face up. She read the message as she stood to greet Patty's husband, Brian, and her two nephews. Their hugs helped refresh Callie's will to move on.

Patty heard the phone sound again to announce the old text. She picked it up, noting who was texting. She then set it back down again on its face. Callie needed time to recharge with family.

#

The crowd was light when Jason and Maya entered The Shack. The establishment was legendary for great bar food, some seafood, and an atmosphere for fun. There was no band for the midweek crowd on a Wednesday night. That would change after Memorial Day, when vacationers and summer workers would fill the place nightly through the summer.

Because the crowd was small, the interior noise was also low. Maya asked to sit inside to enjoy the warmer air than what was blowing outside. They chose an open table by the bar. Jason ordered a beer and water for himself. Maya reluctantly ordered water.

"If we were outside, I could dump my water and fill it with the beer," he observed. "Then we could switch glasses and I could get something else."

Maya gave him a puzzled look to his idea.

"Since when?" she asked, knowing he had no intention to give his beer to her. "You could take the water outside and dump it. Or, you could have just asked for an empty water glass."

"Jesus." he laughed. "I should have kept my mouth shut."

He took a drink as he looked around. When his eyes returned to hers, Maya was staring at him, waiting for her opportunity to ask him for something. Jason regretted joking about the beer he could not legally give her there, knowing he opened the door to something else.

"What?"

"Nothing," she replied while smiling.

Jason did not dig any deeper. Pulling him in was part of her tactic. It often ended with him feeling guilty about something, then giving something else to make it better.

"OK," Maya said, breaking to the anticipation. "What's up with you and Clara? Are we going to see you this summer? It'll be lonely here without anyone else."

Jason waited to respond. He knew Maya had concerns about being in the cottage alone when he was not there. Her concern was also nowhere near his concern that she would be alone when he was not there. They did talk about Maya inviting a friend for the summer. But internships took precedence over her friends' desire to have fun. Jason also considered getting her a dog. But her work schedule and training a puppy would not co-ordinate. Maya also expected to have a roll of visitors plus her sisters and dad through the summer. Jason expected her job would keep her busy, help her meet new friends, and make sleep a priority between days.

"Right now," Jason answered, "Clara and I are just dating exclu-sively. I have no plans beyond that. She makes me happy."

Maya smiled as she heard her dad talk positively about a new woman bringing happiness to his life. The last deep conversa-tion they had about his love life was when she surprised him and Callie the first day after they reunited at his beach house. At first, Maya was furious that her dad was with a married woman at his house. The fact that she was in pajamas, midmorning, raised all sorts of bad thoughts. But Maya quickly came to appreciate and like Callie after talking to her about why she was there. Cal-lie was honest and confused. But she seemed genuine. And her history with her dad certainly made their reconnection decades later meaningful.

"So, you're over Callie," Maya asked, knowing it would sting a little.

Jason took hold of his beer as it was placed on the table. He took a quick swig to calm so that he could answer honestly.

"I don't think that's possible," he answered.

I knew it! Maya thought as she recalled the ten dollars she threw into a pool with her sisters on who their dad would end up with. She thought she had the inside scoop with her early time with Callie. She saw how special she was to her dad. But Maya also liked Clara from the start. Clara just did not have the same glow Callie had. And Callie destroyed her opportunity when she made the decision to take her loser husband back. Maya was getting irritated that criteria outside the scope of the contest caused her to lose the money.

As she continued to think about his reply, Maya remembered him giving the same answer when Callie showed in October. Jason refused to speculate on what he would do if Callie became available because she was married. Maya had always known that Callie was Jason's ONE by the way he joked about her, as his former fiancée, through her life. She started to get concerned that he was closing opportunity too fast when their past showed how quickly the winds could change.

"Is that a problem?" Maya asked.

Jason stood up and walked his water glass to the bar. He asked the bartender to empty it for him. As he sat down, he poured his beer into it. After looking around, he looked to Maya.

"If I give you this beer, can we end this conversation?"

The answer to her question through the beer offer, and his beer, was enough to get her to say yes. As she took her first pull from the glass, she watched her dad start to struggle with his thoughts. She began to regret bringing up the topic.

15

Clara checked her weather app to plan the weekend. Rain was in the forecast to arrive Friday and stay through the weekend. She knew rain often resulted in guests staying in their cabins during the evenings. For her, that translated into more meal orders and deliveries.

Clara took a moment to celebrate that the weekend and following week were all sold out. The final two cabins were rented earlier in the day. She was excited to see the business continue to prosper. Jason's marketing was working.

With the business growth they were experiencing, Clara expected that Jason would want to develop at least one more cabin on the two remaining mountaintop lots. She began to think about their relationship and the lot she owned where she had distributed her husband's ashes. It was time to decide about what to do there for either her, them, or the business.

The main house front porch offered a picture-perfect view of the setting sun beyond the lawn and lily pond. Clara sat in her rocker satisfied that her life, which seemed so desperate when Tom died and the bank was threatening foreclosure, was going to not only work out, but be storybook. Jason and his four daughters were filling a void far beyond her dreams and expectations.

Callie reached down to pet Jason's dog Zoe as she lay peacefully on the floor by her side. Zoe groaned as she always did to appreciate the touches she liked to receive. She always attached herself to Clara when Jason was away. She would, however, and without hesitation, leave her for him when he returned. They were an unbreakable pair. Initially, Clara was jealous of his bond with his dog until their relationship grew exclusive. He was perfect for her.

# # #

Jason set his alarm to wake him early. He had his suitcase packed except for his shaving kit and the clothes he was going to wear on the drive across North Carolina back to Fox Farm. Maya was settled and enjoying her new friends from the lifeguard program. He was comfortable; she was comfortable, which usually meant it was time to leave. To stay would be smothering.

The water was unusually cold and choppy as he headed into the surf wearing his flippers and carrying his lifesaving bullet. He figured he could swim for thirty minutes, take Maya to the coffee shop for a decent breakfast sandwich and coffee, then be on his way back to Asheville. He expected to arrive around five o'clock, just in time for cocktails.

As the waves splashed against his stomach, Jason set his watch timer for thirty minutes. He put the bullet sling over his shoulder and began his Australian crawl out beyond the breakers to the calmer water. Once there, he made a ninety-degree turn north to start his laps.

At the fifteen-minute mark, Jason stopped to take a breather. His body was trying to convince him to quit while his head still knew he had fifteen more minutes to swim. He leaned on his heart to push through to finish his swim as he planned it. As he looked back at the house, he noticed a figure on the bench overlooking the beach. For a moment, he was back on the October day when the image was Callie and she raised her cup to salute his effort. This time, it was Maya telling her dad better you than me. He smiled, knowing that her time was coming to do the same thing in a few hours.

"I can ask the guys if they'd take an old man for the open position they have." Maya laughed as Jason reached the top of the stairs. She then toasted her mug of coffee toward him.

"Did you, by chance, bring me one?" he asked, knowing the answer.

"No," Maya responded as she took a pull to make him jealous. "Is that my job?"

Jason laughed, recalling Callie giving the same answer.

"Give me ten minutes. We can go to the coffee shop before it gets busy."

Jason loaded his bag into the Volvo as Maya started the Wrangler. The weather forecast said the day on the coast was going to be a perfect for topless Jeep cruising. Jason smiled as he watched his youngest daughter adjust her baseball cap and sunglasses for the short drive to the coffee shop. He backed out onto the street and drove away as Maya followed.

The parking lot at the coffee shop had several open slots. That convenience would change as Memorial Day transitioned the community into a summer full of vacation renters. Jason put his arm around Maya to give her a reassuring hug as they entered the shop to order their breakfast and Jason's first coffee of the day.

The always tantalizing display was full of assorted fine pastries, doughnuts, and muffins. Jason's diet had moved away from carbs and sweets until he returned to the shore and restarted swimming. Running the trails at Fox Farm, although challenging, did not burn away the sin foods the way swimming in the ocean did the previous two summers. Jason knew splitting his time between the cabins and the beach was going to be a challenge to keep his weight down without taking out the sweets.

"May I help you?" asked a voice that rose from behind the counter.

The twenty-year-old's eyes grew wide as she looked at Jason, then to Maya. A smile came to her face that puzzled Maya, who looked to her dad for an introduction. Jason shook his head, thinking *This cannot be happening.*

"Hi, Mr. Cartwright," the girl stated. "Hi... Maya."

The girl's voice wavered on Maya, not sure if she was Maya or one of her sisters. Maya again looked to her dad for an assist.

"Lizzie?" Jason questioned with a puzzled look and voice. "How nice to see you here... working."
Jason struggled to push past his surprise to say something positive.

"Yes, I just got this job. I'm on probation for two weeks."

Jason smiled as Lizzie described her status. He then looked for the owner, who was by the cash register.

"Marie!?" he shouted to get her attention. "Lizzie is a friend of the family. She's good folk."

Marie waved as Maya rolled her eyes at his endorsement. She was still searching through her head why the girl looked familiar but could not be placed.

"I just saw your mom and dad last weekend. They didn't say you were working here this summer."

The reference to the weekend put the situation into perspective. Without the baseball cap to hold her hair back, she now recognized Lizzie as Callie's daughter. Maya sighed, enjoying the humor that Callie's daughter had anchored less than a mile from Jason's cottage.

"She doesn't know yet," Lizzie said. "I came with my college housemates for a two-week stay. My mom talked about this shop. I worked at a coffee shop at home and just applied... I really don't want to spend another summer in DC."

Jason looked to Maya, who pointed to her watch. She was losing time to the conversation to eat her breakfast before saying goodbye to him and hitting the guard training and tower.

"Well, I won't tell her." Jason smiled.

He knew he could keep that promise because he felt his connection to Callie had ended. He and Maya both ordered breakfast sandwiches to eat there. Maya added orange juice. They both got large coffees to jumpstart their days. Lizzie followed them to the register, checked them out, and processed the payment with ease. The three said goodbyes at the counter.

"That has to be the most bizarre thing ever," Maya mused as she watched Lizzie wait on other customers.

"She asked a lot of questions when I had dinner with them last summer in Williamsburg. From what I understand, she hates going to Nantucket even though Callie will be there this summer. This may be good for her."

Maya winced at Jason's spin-positive.

"Why here?" she asked. "I mean, the Outer Banks between Corolla to the bottom of Nags Head is, what, twenty-five, thirty miles?

Jason stood to go get their food. He smiled and winked at Lizzie as he took the plates. She gave a small wave to reply.

"This is creepy," Maya added as he sat down.

"Don't worry about it," he answered. "That's something for their family to work out."

"Well, she's not living at the cottage."

Jason stopped as he was about to bite into his sandwich. His eyes shifted from his breakfast to his daughter.

"You don't have to worry about that. Her dad would never let that happen, anyway."

"It's not her dad that I'm worried about saying it's OK."

Jason took a bite of sandwich to think about Maya's clarification. He winked at his daughter as he continued to chew. Lizzie's appearance and job at the beach meant that Callie would likely show up to either fetch her or to visit. He was concerned that that may open more problems for him, and for her, and with Chase and Clara. He also knew he had a seven-hour drive to think about it.

"It'll be fine," he answered. "No to any requests from the Larson family."

Maya could see the gears turning behind his eyes. She knew his promise was just to get out of the conversation. Callie Larson had a power over him that was unbreakable. She knew if Callie asked, or showed, her dad would make an exception. And, if others were staying there too, she could land on a couch.

With breakfast over, Maya and Jason refilled their cups with coffee to start their days that took them in different directions. Jason gave Maya a hug to say goodbye. His standard practice was to wait to watch her drive away. He did it when she headed off to school. He also did it when he visited her at school. It was customary for him to choke up with emotion he never liked to show. Maya found her dad where she expected him to be as she walked across the parking lot.

As Maya neared her car, she noticed a purple Mini Cooper convertible with familiar white Virginia license plates and a large JMU sticker in its back window. She remembered Lizzie's infatuation with her car when she and her sisters dropped off Jason's Jeep in Williamsburg. Lizzie's dad must have come through on his 'I'll see' promise.

Jason responded with a puzzled expression as Maya turned and pointed to the purple Mini. He then smiled when he noticed the car and its JMU sticker, knowing that Lizzie went to James Madison University. When he looked back at Maya, she made a Woo gesture then laughed. Jason toasted his cup as he watched her turn to her car. Maya's backup and exit were faster than Jason would have preferred. He was sad to be saying goodbye to his daughter for a few weeks. He also thought she could be more careful.

"Mr. Cartwright?" Lizzie's voice asked from behind.

Jason turned to Lizzie, who was standing behind him.

"Do you have a minute?"

"Sure," he answered as he tried to assess how long she would need.

His first cup of coffee was already stepping on his bladder. If it was more than to say goodbye, he needed to find relief first.

"It's about my mom," she whispered.

"Absolutely, then," he answered as he handed her his cup. "Find a table where we can chat. I'll be right back."

Jason entered the men's room quickly. As he stopped in front of the mirror, he looked at his reflection. *What the fuck?* he said to himself as he worked through his needs and washed his hands. He was afraid to give this girl any advice on anything. He feared it would be contrary to what Callie would want. He believed, given what he saw in Great Falls, that Callie would want Lizzie there with her. Jason checked his face in the mirror as he dried his hands. He was trying to build the courage to deal with someone else's twenty-year-old daughter.

Lizzie was staring out the window when Jason sat down. He noticed she did not have anything to either drink or eat. He also wondered if she pursued this job knowing they would cross paths at some point.

"It's nice to see you," he opened to ease the moment. "Can I buy you a drink, muffin… anything?"

Lizzie smiled at the offer then declined.

"My mom is going to be mad that I've decided to stay here. But I just can't go home," Lizzie explained. "I was wondering if you could talk to her. It looks like Maya is here for the summer too. Something from you may make it easier to get her to say it's OK."

"Lizzie, I'd love to help you. But you know my story and what's going on. I know your situation at home is uncomfortable. But I think sticking my two cents in anywhere will only hurt your efforts to get permission."

Lizzie forced a smile to show she understood. Both she and Jason knew that getting Callie's permission was going to be a battle. Chase, on the other hand, would likely give it to not have to deal with her in Nantucket.

"I thought I'd ask," Lizzie said as she stood.

Jason watched as the dejected college coed began to realize her days at the beach may be numbered. He remembered Maya's struggle through the last year of his marriage and her hiding in her room during the arguments. He reached into his pocket to retrieve a card from his wallet.

"Here's my card with my cell number and email," Jason explained as he handed it to her. "Text me your number so I have it. I will pick up if you call. My cottage address is on the back. I'll be in and out all summer. Maya is guarding, so she'll be here too. Tell your mom you have a job and saw me with Maya. Let me know how that goes. If she calls me, I'll be your biggest advocate to stay."

Lizzie's face lit with the new hope Jason just instilled in her. As he stood, she gave him a hug to say thank you and goodbye.

"Thank you so much," she replied.

"Call me if you need me. I now know a lot of people here. They're all good people."

Jason waved as Lizzie turned to go back behind the counter. As he looked to the door, he caught a look from the coffee shop's owner, Marie. She sensed drama in Lizzie's life, which made her reluctant to hire her. But Jason's endorsement, and Lizzie's goodbye hug, gave her confidence that Lizzie was going to be fine.

"Marie, see you in a few weeks," Jason said as he waved goodbye.

"OK, Jason," she replied as he walked out the door. "Remember, come earlier, and come often when you do."

#

A flash filled the office, followed by a clap of thunder that rattled the windows. The storms the weather service said were coming to start the rainy weekend had arrived. Clara moved the curtain to watch the sheets of rain pound the water and lily pads on the pond. Deluges like this one tended to raise the pond level to touch the driveway before receding back down to normal levels. Zoe curled at her feet against the wall.

"It's OK, girl," Clara said as she kneeled to pet her shadow. "Your dad's driving here now. He'll be here soon."

Clara returned to look out the window. A small river was flowing down the lane from the Flying Dutchman, across the main drive, and down into the pond. The cloud cover had erased most of the daylight as the thickness of the rain limited visibility beyond the front gate.

Clara checked her watch as she saw a gray blur with red brake lights slow to turn on to the driveway. Guests were due to arrive. But the car was coming from the wrong direction. As the glow of its halogen headlights turned toward the house, the arriving car became a BMW sedan driven by what appeared to be a woman.

Clara straightened her blouse and moved to the front desk to receive the arriving guest. As she readied herself, Zoe repositioned at her feet behind the desk. A bright flash filled the room, followed by a crushing boom, causing the power to go out. The door flew open as a woman stumbled into the room, frightened by being between her car and the porch when the lightning flashed.

"Are you OK?" Clara asked as she ran to help.

The woman sat on the wood bench by the desk, noticeably startled but beginning to pull herself back together.

"I'm fine, just frightened," the woman replied. "Is it supposed to be like this all weekend?"

"No," Clara responded. "Once this front moves through, it'll be rainy, but not like this."

"Good," she replied. "I don't expect to be going anywhere. This is supposed to be a romantic weekend."

Clara smiled as the woman stood to approach the desk. Clara's laptop was running on battery. The blue screen illuminated her face as she looked at the list of reservations and cabins they were assigned to.

"Last name?" Clara asked.

"Shallot," Sarah replied. "Sarah Shallot."

Clara rolled the cursor down the screen to Sarah's reservation.

"You'll be in one of my favorite cabins." Clara smiled as she clicked to record Sarah's arrival on her screen. "You're in the Flying Dutchman, which is where we hang out when it's not rented."

"That must be nice," Sarah replied as she handed Clara a credit card to secure charges for food and drink. "You can have the run of the place. Do it in every cabin."

Clara smiled at Sarah's attempt at a joke. How she said it made it sound dirty.

"You'll love it. It's very romantic," Clara answered as she returned Sarah's card.

"I hope so. I've got a surprise for my fiancé," she answered. "I'm finally pregnant!"

Sarah's elation to share the news with someone showed in her smile and step. Callie's face lit as she watched Sarah revel in her joy.

"Well, congratulations. Normally, we'd send champagne up for celebrations. But you can't—"

"Drink," Sarah finished for her. "Nope, not any more for a while. I just found out. So, I'm still really giddy."

"That's better than champagne!"

"I know. I can't wait to tell him. He'll be here around nine o'clock. I'd like to order food to be delivered."

Clara encouraged Sarah to order from the main house using her cell phone. She handed her the book of menus to see her choices. Sarah complimented the quality of the food options. She ordered a bottle of bourbon from the main house's supply to take with her. If she could not drink to celebrate, Chase certainly could.

"My fiancé, can he drive straight to the cabin? Or does he need to check in too?"

"He's fine as long as you give him directions. We do have cameras outside all the cabins for security. You have two parking spaces. So, you should be fine."

Sarah smiled at Clara's response. The security cameras made her feel more secure with their cabin in the woods.

"Oh," Clara asked, "I forgot to ask you how you heard about us."

"Sure. A friend stayed here last fall. Said it was really elegant and fun. I've had you bookmarked since then. We were supposed to boat this weekend but got washed out with the rain. So, here we are!"

Clara smiled as Sarah looked back to the rain outside. The heavy storms had passed, leaving a consistent but manageable rain in its wake. Clara pointed to the road back to the Flying Dutchman. She told Sarah to drive slowly so her car did not bottom out as it hit some of the bumps in the road. Clara watched Sarah work her way through the rain back to her car. As she backed away to turn, Clara waved and smiled.

"Now, that's just the best news I've heard all day," Clara said to herself as she petted the top of Zoe's head.

Sarah's brake lights lit as she slowed to make the turn back to the Flying Dutchman. As Clara watched the BMW disappear into the trees and fog, she was jealous that Sarah had such a huge joy to announce to the man who loved her. She then looked back at the road for Jason to arrive.

16

Clara had parked the farm's pristine 1992 Jeep Grand Wagoneer in the shed to keep it from being damaged by the storm. Over the past few years, several heavy thunderstorms produced marble-size hail that would cover the grass like snow and dent anything metal left out in the open. She knew Jason would be upset if he arrived to find hail dimples on his prized Jeep that could have been prevented by simply parking the truck in the shed.

Jason's drive across the state slowed as he entered the weather front that was working its way up western North Carolina. What started in sunshine at the beach was now under the dense, dark cloud cover that was bringing a deluge that showed no signs of letting up. Blackburn Road was darker and harder to drive than the highway because of its two opposing lanes and tight tree lines. Jason was happy to see the tree line break and open to the farm.

As he passed the front of the property, he signaled to turn through the two stone pillars that said he was home. The main house had a yellow glow of lights coming from inside, which was unusual for six o'clock. But the darkness of the storm made it necessary. Jason was glad to see that the farm still had power. The generator he ordered months earlier for this type of weather was scheduled to arrive later in the spring.

Clara saw the lights shine on the shed as the Volvo pulled to a stop in the drive next to the kitchen. She was preparing the wicker baskets to deliver food and was glad to have an extra pair of hands. Zoe stood and ran to the door when she heard the car stop. She had an ear for his car that would alert and excite her to his arrival long before anyone else heard anything. She was ready to see and change masters.

Clara stayed on the covered porch as Jason hustled up the walkway with his suitcase. He looked tired from the weather-heavy drive. She smiled as he gave her a weary look and kissed him the moment he stepped onto the porch.

"I missed you," she said as a tingle went through her body.

Jason smiled, happy to have such a warm welcome.

"It's so good to be home," he answered. "What a crazy day."

Jason kissed Clara again before kneeling down to hug his waiting four-legged companion. Her wiggling body was shaking the porch. Their week of separation was finally over.

"You're just in time to help deliver the food," Clara said as she turned to walk into the kitchen.

"I'd rather have a drink," he replied as he followed.

Jason stopped and looked at the twelve baskets waiting to be delivered. He knew there were usually only six. But the rain always meant people stayed in for the evening. The service charge on the food was the only incentive he had to be happy to see all the deliveries.

"Any of this ours?" he asked, opening the first one to see.

Clara smiled as she pointed to two rib-eye steaks warming to room temperature in a cast -iron skillet. Beside the stove was a small pile of red potatoes and a salad.

"I'm making you dinner," she answered as she leaned her body against his.

Jason closed his eyes to enjoy her warmth. He then kissed her on the forehead as he kept her close with a hug.

"Divine... What?" He laughed while struggling to think. "I need an 'I' word."

Clara's work-through of divine intervention being why they met, then divine inspiration to give her the courage to share her feelings with him, was pressing Jason for the right 'I' word to use for the perfect dinner with the perfect woman.

"Intuition," Clara answered. "We're one and the same, now."

Jason smiled without acknowledging it as perfect, like he usually would. Her definition dampened the humor in her choice of words.

"We're going to need more 'I' words," he commented as he let go and started toward the waiting baskets.

# # #

The baskets were carefully loaded into the back of the Volvo. Special care was taken to ensure easy access to each basket as they arrived at each cabin. With the rain still falling, Jason and Clara chose the Volvo because its large, flip-up tailgate provided good cover for whoever had to get the basket out.

The transfers all occurred without problems. Most guests opened their door to help when the Volvo appeared in their cabin's driveway. For guests that did not appear, the meals were placed in the secure holding box that Clara's husband, Tom, built. A marker was flipped to say that dinner was inside. Each delivery also got a knock on the door. The dinners all came with warming instructions to get the food back up to optimum temperatures.

With only one basket left, Jason pulled over the hill to see his favorite cabin occupied. The BMW that Clara watched disappear back into the drive had made it there safely. The yellow glow of lights said that someone was home.

Sarah heard the grind of the gravel as the Volvo came to a stop. Clara jumped out to deliver the last basket of the night that was sitting on the seat behind her. Since the rain was in a lull, Jason got out to stretch his legs and to look around.

"This is an interesting story," Clara said as she walked to the door.

Jason turned to look at her after studying the car with the South Carolina plates. The five series BMW was a sedan he always admired. But its lack of utility for a dog forced him to drive SUVs until he bought the Volvo wagon.

"This place is ripe for a mini-series." He chuckled, thinking about all the stories that could be written about Fox Farm cabin visitors and its surrounding community.

As he watched Clara start to open the box, the door rattled open. Sarah's face, originally loaded with excitement, emptied as she saw her visitor was Clara delivering dinner.

"Oh," she said with a disappointed tone.

"You thought I was your fiancé, didn't you?" Clara qualified.

"Yes."

Clara looked to Jason as he walked toward the door. Hearing his steps, Sarah turned to see who else was making deliveries with Clara. She was impressed with Jason's appearance as more polished than what she expected for a delivery driver. The Volvo Cross Country station wagon also did not fit the mold.

"Sarah," Clara interjected, "this is Jason. He is the owner of Fox Farm."

Sarah smiled as Jason approached her. His lean build and perfect salt-n-pepper look was highly attractive. She extended her hand to meet his.

"I'm happy to meet you," Sarah said before Jason could speak.

"Thank you. Me too," he answered. "How's everything in the Dutchman for you?"

"It's so perfect," she answered. "My fiancé is going to love it."

Jason looked to Clara with a smile. He always enjoyed hearing great first impressions.

"That's great to hear. Let us know if there's anything we can do to make it better," he replied before he started backing toward the car.

Clara looked to Sarah, who appeared happier than she was after she opened the door.

"Can I tell him your news?"

"It's going to be public as of tonight," Sarah answered. "So, go ahead."

Clara turned to Jason, excited to tell him about what she learned.

"I'm pregnant," Sarah blurted out, unable to hold it in.

Jason's reaction was startled before relaxing to a smile. By his gauge, Sarah read to be about forty years old.

"That's fantastic," he replied as Clara reached to hug Sarah to eliminate the awkwardness.

"We usually—"

Clara raised her hand to stop him. She explained that she told Sarah about the champagne tradition. Jason then offered it again as a take-home memento to be enjoyed later. If anything was to be celebrated, expecting a child was at the top of his list. Sarah smiled and accepted his offer.

Clara carried the basket inside for Sarah while Jason remained outside. When she returned to the Volvo, Jason had turned it around to face back toward the main house with the passenger door open and facing the cabin.

"Sarah told me that this will be her first child," Clara said as she buckled her seat belt. "Her fiancé has three from his former marriage. That's when I told her you had four daughters."

"What'd she say to that?"

"She laughed. She also asked if we were together. Said she felt a vibe."

Sarah waved goodbye through the door as they drove out the

driveway. Her thought was how nice it would be to have a simple life like theirs, away from everything in the mountains, to raise a child. Jason's look, polish, and appreciation for European motorcars showed that his life could fit Chase too.

# # #

Chase downshifted the Mustang to slow for the turn onto the property through the two stone pillars. When Sarah texted him the plans and address of the property, his first thought was that she had rented a rustic cabin that would be dirty and uncomfortable. His first impression, however, from the road and through a little drizzle, was positive.

The original farmhouse presented well behind a large lily pond, all surrounded by manicured landscape. The concise tree line that marked the perimeter of the property front with its neatly cut driveways, each marked with small white direction signs, added elegance. The property reminded him of a golf resort minus the golf course and oversized clubhouse.

Sarah's instructions were to turn right at the first road back into the trees to the cabin called The Flying Dutchman. Chase liked the name. It was strong and presented character. On the first bottoming of his car on the gravel road, he also remembered Sarah's caution to drive slowly on the driveway back to the cabin.

As he came over the hill to the cabin, he was excited to see her BMW parked outside along with the warm yellow glow of lights coming through the window. The cabin presented much differently than he expected. It had a warm, welcoming aura. He was happy to have arrived.

Sarah heard his car on the gravel. She bounded out of the cabin as Chase grabbed his weekend bag. As he walked toward her, she jumped into his arms to kiss him hello. A smile came to his face to get such an excited welcome. With the seclusion of the cabin, and the rain that was staying for the weekend, Chase expected that her welcome meant a lot of alone time, together, in bed.

"Well?"

"It's fantastic," Chase answered as he walked into the living area.

"I know," she replied, excited to hear his approval. "The bedroom and shower are all nice too."

Chase walked to the deck to check its size, amenities, and treetop views.

"I hope we get to use this," he commented as he turned.

Chase's concern that Sarah had rented a dump was replaced by a new excitement to spend the weekend in country luxury. After the weekend wedding, fight with Callie, and collision with both Jason and Mark, he needed a few days to decompress and heal his soreness.

"We have it until Monday morning."

Chase smiled at the thought of not having to lose Sunday evening. The drive back to Spartanburg was just over an hour. He had everything set to go for the following week. And, since nothing in the campaign was either left open or to chance, he looked to the bar for a soother.

"I've had this before," Chase said as he looked at the bottle of Roughrider bourbon Sarah bought at the main house. "It's from New York."

Chase paused as he remembered his last taste back in July at his mother-in-law's home after she died. He needed its support to push through his negotiation with Callie to let him back into their marriage. He poured himself a double over ice as he continued to study the bottle. After taking a sip, he looked at it again while expressing his appreciation for its contents.

"The woman that checked me in said that it's the owner's favorite… for now."

"It's good," Chase answered. "Do you want some wine? Do we have wine?"

Sarah hesitated as she beamed for Chase to notice. The news was pressing to explode out of her.

"I have mine in the fridge," she answered as she walked toward the kitchen. She wanted something appropriate to toast their loving creation. She pulled a flavored bottle of Pellegrino water from the house stock that was in the fridge.

Chase took another sip as he read the Teddy Roosevelt association to the bourbon whisky he was drinking. He took a picture of the label with his phone. He then walked to the deeply cushioned loveseat where both Callie and Clara had spent time positioning for Jason ten months earlier. He sat on the corner where Callie was when she clearly staked her claim for Jason. The couch was comfortable and perfect for a romantic snuggle.

Sarah walked around the table with a tea glass full of water. As she sat down, she smiled as she presented her glass for a toast.

"To finally being together," she said as Chase brought his glass to hers.

He noticed that the glass was not the wine glass he expected. After he touched glasses to toast the start of their romantic weekend, he took a pull of bourbon. The mellow burn across his gums felt right as he watched Sarah take a sip of water from her glass.

"Are you not drinking tonight?" he asked. "We aren't going anywhere."

Sarah smiled as she took his bourbon and put both their glasses on the table. She then moved closer to take his hands in hers. After a pause to enjoy the excitement that was building in her, she shifted her eyes from their joined hands to his.

"I've got some news," Sarah said, trying to hold back her smile.

"Oh no," Chase responded.

"I'm pregnant," she exclaimed in an elated voice. "We're going to have a baby."

Sarah jumped onto him to celebrate the news. Her elation gave her such a high that she did not notice Chase's cold reaction. He was only a supporting touch to keep her from falling. Their emotions were on different ends of the earth. Sarah was surprised and upset that he was showing no joy for the amazing life event they were about to share together. Obviously, their earlier discussions about having a child together were just words.

"What's wrong?" she asked. "Why aren't you happy?"

"Oh my God, Sarah," Chase said while releasing her to stand. "This is really bad timing."

"Chase, I'm almost forty. 'Timing' is ending for me to do this."

Chase broke his stare on her as he ran his hands through his hair and walked to stare out into the rain.

"I thought you'd be excited."

Chase slumped as he closed his eyes to a blank mind. He was feeling a slight joy in knowing that he and Sarah had reached the point of joining together. But that one bright spot was quickly overwhelmed by the realization that a baby with her would create pressure on him to follow through on his commitment to marry her. And she did not know his divorce was not only not final, but not happening. Sarah handed him his bourbon to calm his nerves.

"I thought you'd be as excited as I am," she whispered, near tears.

Chase took a pull from his glass, then forced a smile.

"I am, sweetie," he answered. "It's a shocker, for sure. And I'm tired from the drive. I didn't even know we were trying."

Chase moved to touch his forehead to hers. His eyes were as sincere as his words. Sarah's acceptance was warm and understanding, despite his reaction being contrary to what she expected.

"We weren't," she answered.

Sarah's comment brought back a funny memory with Callie when she announced she was pregnant when they were not trying. The bright side was that they no longer had to careful to not get pregnant. Chase's expression faded as he thought about those laughs with her over twenty years ago.

"Well," Chase stated, "lots to think about and to plan for."

His mind was now working opposite to Sarah's. Chase was already processing how to deal with the news to keep it secret until Callie's mother's estate settled. Her dad's inheritance was left to both of them as a married couple. He expected that Carolyn would not have thought to make changes in her will until their divorce was final. That was how her family operated. And Callie had made no mention of it.

Sarah, on the other hand, was in the process of planning her new life and home with Chase. They had talked about living in Charleston. It was closer to his campaign network. He could always fly to DC to meet with the RNC, as needed. Her vision was a traditional Southern clapboard house with a large wraparound porch. She knew what consultants Chase's field earned, which could afford that lifestyle. His mention of his ex-wife's family wealth added to her expectation that he had resources for her to live on. Sarah smiled as she watched her love finish his bourbon as he stared off into the treetops.

The water from the rain elevated the pond level to the main drive. Jason stepped out onto the front porch during a lull to assess the situation. The tree that fell the summer before was left to decorate the gap in the tree line created by the spillway. Its leafless skeleton created an artistic draw that Jason and Clara both liked. But after every hard rain, debris that washed into and through the pond got stuck in the tree to back the pond water up to the driveway.

Clara watched through the kitchen window as Jason and Zoe walked to the shed. She had an eerie feeling that she had lived this before. When he emerged with Tom's refurbished chainsaw, she immediately dried her hands to intercede on what she knew he was doing.

"No way," she declared as she charged out of the side door to intercept him.

Jason increased his pace to be past her interception point to stop him. They both started to laugh as Clara started to walk faster too.

"Jason," she declared as she stopped. "Don't."

Clara was giving him the opportunity to keep going with a wave and smart comment. But the sincerity in her voice and the look of worry on her face made him stop.

"You know what happened last time you tried this," she pleaded.

Jason smiled at the thought, recalling it was the first time he looked at Clara as a love interest. She was soaked, standing in pond water with debris in her hair and on her body. She radiated not only from how she looked but also to how she reacted when he pulled her under the water.

"We can do it again," he said with a devilish smirk.

"Not a chance," she answered. "I'll let you fall in by yourself this time. In fact, I'm not even going to watch."

Jason stayed silent as he used a puzzled face expression to tell her he knew she would be watching. He knew she wanted to be able to say I told you so.

"Go," she finally surrendered. "Just don't hurt yourself."

Jason stood taller as she gave her permission.

"I have a plan with just one cut," he said with a smile. "I'm just going to walk around the pond, this time, to cut the other side. The pond backup should push the tree and all that crap caught in it off the spillway."

Clara answered with a blind wave as she walked back to the house. The sound of the chainsaw running would be her sign to worry. When it stopped would be her time to check on him and the results. Why men were so pig-headed in their approach to property projects continued to baffle her. The pond would recede back to normal in a few days.

# # #

Chase walked out onto the deck to survey the grounds around the Flying Dutchman. The floor and furniture were still wet from the heavy rain.

As he walked the deck from end to end, the quality of the construction combined with the furniture continued to impress him. When he looked to the deck's hidden corner, he was surprised and excited to see the hot tub. He then shifted his eyes to the sky, hopeful that the rain would stop long enough to enjoy it later.

Sarah slid the glass door open to follow him onto the deck. She was happy that his initial reaction to her news had reversed course to excitement. She knew he had a game face he could put forward to convince others that he was for something, when he was actually thinking of a way to kill it. She had the same ability. Her comfort came in the belief that she knew him well enough to read when he was faking, and when he was real.

"We need to go get some things if we're going to stay in," Sarah said as he continued to look around.

"We can just order meals," Chase replied. "I'm really digging this cabin."

"I need to get things. I need to have good breakfasts now. Plus, we need munchies, sodas, and other things."

Chase smiled as he looked at Sarah in a different light. He was beginning to see the radiance that came with pregnancy that he used to love in Callie. He was never certain if it was because of a hormonal change, or just an attitude adjustment that came with the expectation of becoming a parent. It did not matter; he was excited to see it in Sarah.

"Let's go now before it rains again."

The black BMW came to a stop where the lane from the cabin

intersected with the farm's main driveway. Chase noticed the barren tree hanging over the pond's end while a property worker walked toward it carrying a chainsaw. His gray sweatshirt and baseball cap obscured Chase's ability to see the man clearly. But the man looked to be about his age, fit ,and ready to attack the tree that was backing up the pond.

"I think that's the owner," Sarah commented as they turned to head to Blackburn Road. "I met him last night. He's about your age and has four daughters."

Chase did not respond to Sarah's comment as he slowed to watch the man approach the tree.

"The woman that checked me in is living with him. They're not married because she introduced him as the owner. When I asked, she told me they just recently fell in love. She has no children, so his four daughters creates an instant family of women for her. Isn't that romantic?"

Chase remained quiet as the car approached the stone pillars and front gate. The male gene that always made men stop to watch manual labor was kicking in to see the tree cut and fall. Chase watched as Jason continue his walk toward the spillway and the fallen tree. He saw Zoe exit the pond with a stick that she dropped at his feet. Jason patted on her head and pointed to get her to move away. When she refused, he picked up the stick and threw it like a frisbee back into the water. Zoe took three steps before leaping into the pond to paddle to retrieve the stick.

"Now, that's the kind of dog I'd like to have," Chase remarked, thinking about how Molly avoided play and water.

"We can get you one," Sarah replied. "It'd be perfect for our child to grow up with."

Chase smiled his agreement as he took his foot off the brake. It appeared the man they were watching had more planning to do before making his final decision on where to cut. Chase drove Sarah's BMW through the gate and turned away from Jason to go explore and buy supplies.

17

Maya began to slow the Jeep down as she approached the cottage. She was getting used to driving Jason's Wrangler as a fun alternative to her Mini Cooper convertible. But with gas fillups being more frequent and expensive, she was not sure if her dad would notice and be upset with her. As she approached the house, she noticed a colorless Mini Cooper convertible slowly rolling down the road toward her. The glare of the sun was overwhelming her ability to see colors of anything shiny in front of her.

Noticing other Mini Coopers was something that developed only after she got hers. All of a sudden, the NC State campus, and city of Raleigh, seemed to be full of other Minis. Anticipating her turn into the cottage's driveway, Maya did not give the car another look until it was about to pass her. She downshifted into second gear as she prepared to turn into the cottage driveway. She could see her car parked underneath on the left side of the cottage. The right was unoccupied and open for the Jeep. As she started to turn the wheel, Maya looked at the Mini Cooper that had changed from no color to purple. Her stomach pitted as she looked to the driver clad in gold Ray-Ban aviators leaning into her steering wheel with her mouth open. Maya stood on her brakes to stop.

The reaction time of both drivers stopped both cars past each other. Maya checked both ways to ensure no one was coming. She then backed up to Lizzie's car. Her ask was going to see if she needed anything. Her intent was to bust her for snooping.

"Hey," Maya said as Lizzie turned toward her. "Pull into the driveway."

Maya's workday was over and she had free time. She pulled into the Jeep's usual parking lot as Lizzie turned around to follow. As Lizzie parked the car behind the Jeep, Maya could see her assessing the cottage for its size and appeal. As she got out, Maya turned to invite her up to the deck for a cold drink.

Lizzie followed Maya up the stairs while engaged in small talk about the coffee shop and Maya's job as a lifeguard. They entered through the windowless side door into the air conditioning that felt good to both of them. Maya pulled a Diet Pepsi from the refrigerator and offered Lizzie a drink. She added there were White Claws for cocktail hour later if she wanted to hang out. Lizzie accepted the Diet Pepsi as she studied the refined interior of Jason's cottage.

"This is super nice," Lizzie commented as she looked around.

Her eyes focused on the decorative features, art, and quality of everything that was there. Her mind thought of her mom there for periods of time in the fall and last summer.

"My dad's all about simple," Maya answered. "Simple, but nice."

Lizzie smiled as she thought about the houses her family rented in Nantucket. They were big and nice. But they lacked all feeling of home that this cottage seemed to radiate.

"You must love it here," she answered.

Maya directed Lizzie out onto the deck that was covered by a pergola Jason had installed for shade. The upright slats cut the sun enough to kill most of its heat while letting some light through. The pergola provided needed shade without darkening the living room. It also was not susceptible to being blown away like a parachute in a storm. Jason made a special effort to ensure his girls understood the reason for its design.

"This is our favorite spot," Maya said as they approached the bench overlooking the surf.

The house where Lizzie was staying sat a row back and across a street from the ocean. Its view of the water was obstructed by large oceanfront homes that were newer and taller than the Cartwright cottage. Lizzie stopped to look up and down the entire coastline. A jealousy developed in her that her family should have a house like this too.

"I could live here forever," she said without thinking.

Maya laughed as she pulled towels from the holding bin under the bench.

"I thought that too. But winter here is empty and can be brutal. I think a six and six, like my dad has now in the mountains, is perfect."

Lizzie continued to study the seascape, watching the few beach walkers that were present in May. Maya was happy to have one-upped, and to be the envy of the spoiled rich girl, given the expression she was showing.

"Want to go for a walk?" Maya asked, knowing that adding that the house was thirty unobstructed yards of sand from the ocean would add to Lizzie's envy of the cottage.

As they made their way through the sand to touch the water, Maya noticed a quiet, withdrawn aspect of Lizzie that did not seem to jibe with her outgoing personality. The fact that she caught Lizzie snooping on the cottage was not a surprise. She would have done the same thing if in northern Virginia to snoop on Callie's home. That goal also assumed she could get past the guard at the front gate she thought would be there.

As Lizzie stayed quiet, Maya was happy to see a familiar figure approaching.

"Hey, Maya," Rebecca stated as she walked to meet the girls. "How's the guarding going?"

Rebecca's face was excited to see Maya and to study her new friend.

"It's tough." Maya laughed. "I'm not so sure I'll do it again."

Rebecca smiled at the confession. She knew the demands of the job and training, having worked the same job in her college years. She also knew Jason pushed Maya to apply, then pulled a few strings to get her the job. Maya knew that quitting was not an option. Her dad, as he did in soccer, wanted her to commit to excel.

"You'll be fine," Rebecca answered as she touched her shoulder for support. "Your dad is proud of you."
Rebecca threw in the second half to both encourage Maya and to buy time to move her eyes to Lizzie for an introduction.

"Hi, I'm Rebecca," she finally said while extending her hand.

"Oh," Maya answered. "This is Callie... I mean, Lizzie Larson."

As Rebecca reached out, she processed Maya's mix-up. Her first look to Maya was surprise before she smiled at Lizzie. Knowing who Lizzie was exposed her resemblance to her mother. She was an almost perfect photocopy, just younger.

"I know your mom," Rebecca said to ease the moment. "She's great. How is she?"

Lizzie smiled at Rebecca's warmth as pressure starting building inside her to not say anything that could hurt either of them.

"My mom is fine. She's in DC," Lizzie answered, knowing to leave out mention of her dad.

"Well, you tell her Rebecca says hi and that we expect to see her this summer."

The conversation stalled as all three looked at each other. Each felt an awkwardness in the situation.

"Well, Maya... and Lizzie, I'm going to head on with my walk. You enjoy yours."

Rebecca touched Maya again as she left. Lizzie noticed the friendly affection between her dad's friend and daughter. It was not the type of relationship she had with anyone on Nantucket, outside of family.

As Rebecca walked out of earshot, Maya and Lizzie continued their walk in the opposite direction.

"I met your mother here," Maya said, knowing it was the direction Lizzie wanted. "It was the October weekend that she first showed up. I came in the next morning, unannounced, which really threw a wrench into everything."

Maya smiled, recalling her dad's initial reaction to her arrival. His nervousness and stiffness, and not knowing what to say, was annoying then, but it was funny now. The ensuing hours of discovery that Callie was married, and not believing she was there for anything other than an affair, were brutal. But through talking with her, Maya grew to appreciate Callie's situation and needs. She had just watched the same thing unfold a few years earlier with her own parents.

"I think that was the first lie my mom ever told me," Lizzie remarked as she stared at the sand. "She said that she was visiting an old friend from Cleveland."

Maya smiled at a thought that immediately came to mind. It was not a complete lie. Her thought was also the same comment Jason made to Callie when she told him after it happened.

"If it makes you feel any better, my dad struggled that whole weekend. He was a mess when I arrived. He expected nothing to evolve out of it. She was married. He had to accept that he blew it. Which, by the way, we both should celebrate, because, had they married, neither of us would be here talking."

Lizzie smiled at the comment. Maya's thinking was way ahead and much deeper than hers.

"My dad also said it didn't matter what he wanted," Maya continued. "Your mom was married, and the decision on that had to happen first. It was a really healthy weekend for him, feelings-wise."

"My dad said my mom was down here banging her old fiancé."

Maya stopped as she thought through the words Lizzie's father used.

"One, I don't even want to think about that... ever... with anyone..." Maya joked to lighten the conversation. "Two, that didn't happen. That weekend was exponentially deeper than a fling between two old loves. They were both reeling in their situations and trying to find answers. I left like three hours after I arrived to give them space."

Lizzie peered over to show she was listening and believed Maya's explanation.

"I just can't see my mom and dad apart."

"I'm not going to lie," Maya replied. "It sucks. And, if either of them pairs up with someone that you don't like, it's worse. I didn't talk to my dad for months. My Mini Cooper is a direct result of his guilt. My sisters had more boring cars in college. But I have to say, it does work out."

Lizzie listened as her eyes shifted to the waves. A smile appeared on her face when she aligned Maya's reason for getting a Mini Cooper convertible to hers. Not long after their grandmother's funeral, her dad bought her a Mini convertible and her brother a Jeep Unlimited that was newer, and more dressed up, than Jason's.

"Does your mom have a new boyfriend?"

"Yup," Maya answered. "Pretty darn fast after the divorce too."

"That's hard."

"It's no different than what you felt with my dad. So... I get it."

"I hope my mom lets me stay," Lizzie confessed. "Could I hang out with you guys when your sisters come?"

Maya smiled at Lizzie's innocence, envisioning her indoctrination with Rachel's Molotov cocktail margarita happy hour.

"Any time." She laughed. "Just come... but if you drink, you have to stay. My dad insists on that. Uber is not an option either."

Lizzie smiled to the bonus offer of staying over. She remembered the fun the sisters had together when they delivered the Jeep to her grandmother's house and when they drove away rocking after her grandmother's funeral and burial. The four sisters were a tight group who enjoyed each other. Lizzie did not have that with her brothers. Her mom had that with her Aunt Patty.

The girls made their turn to start back to the cottage. Maya invited Lizzie to stay to split a pizza and to talk. What both discovered about the other was how similar they were, despite growing up in different houses with much different dynamics. Both Lizzie and Maya said goodbye, thinking they had made a new friend. Maya was hopeful Lizzie would be granted permission to stay. Lizzie was looking forward to more fun at the Cartwright cottage that her mother visited and was aptly called Serenity Now.

# # #

Chase's radio silence all week was unusual. There were times in the past when he went silent for a few days. But six days was pushing the limit, even during his most stressful and busy campaigns.

We need to talk

The words appeared on the dashboard screen in Sarah's car as they drove. The arrival of the text interrupted the Spotify playlist Chase was playing after his phone automatically paired to her car. He immediately regretted letting that happen.

"What's going on with her?" Sarah asked suspiciously.

Chase shifted his body back into his seat as he shook his head. He pressed the play button to continue the music.

"Something with Will and New York City," Chase lied to put blame on Callie.

"You going to answer?" Sarah asked, anxious to get more details.

"Siri? Text Callie," Chase stated to pull up his iPhone assistant.

"What message would you like to send?" Siri asked in a British female accent.

Chase looked at Sarah and smiled.

"Your accent is sexier," he mumbled before dictating. "Let's talk later unless it's an emergency. Period. Send."

Call me when free

Chase exhaled, relieved that Callie did not write something he did not want Sarah to see.

"I'll deal with it later." he said as he patted Sarah's leg.

Sarah took his hand to hold as they approached the country market. The trip to the store got delayed while the rain stayed away, allowing them to visit Lake Lure and to have a healthy lunch that someone else prepared. Sarah had already ordered their dinner that was scheduled to be delivered around six-thirty. She knew they had time and could be late because of the farm's delivery system.

"I wonder if they have any real moonshine," Chase said as he put the car into park.

"That's healthy," Sarah replied. "You definitely should ask."

# # #

The water receded to normal levels soon after the tree fell behind the spillway. The single cut Jason completed to separate the trunk from its base was enough to enable the water pressure to work its magic. Clara was relieved that his project ended safely and worked. She watched nervously as he followed the tree into the void behind the spillway to cut it up. In her opinion, she did not think it was necessary. Jason later insisted it was. Clara let it go without objection, using her boys with their toys reason to worry but not care.

"I have to admit," Clara said as she carried two teas out, "you did a good job."

Jason accepted the compliment without the explanation or guilt he wanted to throw for doubting him. They sat on two rockers next to each other and started a synchronized sway back and forth. Jason pulled his phone from his pocket to check his calendar.

"I forgot that production scout is coming to visit this week," he commented as he double checked the date.

"I didn't," Clara replied. "We have to plan the tour with the cabins filling during the week."

"Yeah, and show them the views from up top," Jason added, referring to the lots still not developed. "And they'll need location suggestions around here for whatever they need to do."

"I hope it works. It'll be great to get the publicity. Sort of like that *Dirty Dancing* place in Virginia."

Jason had thought about the similarities many times. Rumor was the lodge in *Dirty Dancing* was located somewhere near Blacksburg and Virginia Tech. After several unsuccessful attempts to get Siri to research it for him, Clara insisted he quit to keep from getting frustrated and angry at his phone assistant.

"The only problem is that if the story location isn't here, then people will have to dig into the credits to find us."

Clara smiled at her marketing man, who was missing the obvious.

"Or we use it in our marketing to build interest, intrigue, and rumors about our cabins being part of the movie."

Jason smiled as he heard Clara's thoughts.

"You're becoming very good at manipulative marketing," he said as he studied her expression. "I'm beginning to worry that you're starting to manipulate me."

Clara laughed at the comment. He was a good teacher. But her tactics started long before now. She would say she started going for him just after their swim in the pond when his first attempt to clear the tree failed.

Zoe's head popped up from her resting spot in front of the rockers when the BMW pulled into the driveway. Clara looked over to check if the car was unfamiliar as Jason watched Zoe tune in to the arrival.

"That's a good dog, Zo Zo," he said before he turned to look at Clara.

He noticed Clara had a puzzled look on her face as she continued to look at the empty driveway. He knew from her expression that she was mentally processing what she saw in her head. Where she was looking no longer mattered.

"What's got you thinking?" he asked to pull her back.

"Nothing," Clara answered after finally discarding a wild thought she just had.

"Maybe we should start getting things pulled together for dinner deliveries," Jason said as he stood and offered his hand to her.

Clara rose slowly as she mentally reran the image of the car driver. Although the glass was tinted, the image she saw was familiar. She tried to place it with guests from the past, which was not successful. Sarah said neither of them had visited Fox Farm before. The image from the car, that was stuck in her head, was going to continue to bug her.

18

The glow from the seventy-five-inch television was the only light falling out into the darkness from the Larsen house. Callie was curled on the couch with Molly beside her. The program on the screen was white noise and of no consequence to her. Her glass of wine was half full, just as it was when she poured it two hours earlier.

After his quick, curt response to her text, Callie expected that Chase would have either followed up with her by text or a phone call before dinner time. She expected his dinner would be occupied with either his client or potential funders. In the past, those meetings ended by nine o'clock so that Chase's guests could get home to their families. With the clock in her family room showing ten o'clock, Callie concluded that a call from him was not coming. She turned the TV off to head to bed.

Callie was halfway through her routine of washing to prepare for bed when she stopped. Her routine included washing her face with a special cleanser recommended by a dermatologist, followed by head-to-toe lotion on her body. Her regimen, that required effort and was often teased by Chase, had worked compared to her friends who were experiencing dramatic skin challenges as they hit their late forties and fifties. Her mother's demand that they limit their sun exposure as children and young adults set in enough that she not only continued it through adulthood but embedded the same awareness in her kids too.

The image Callie saw looking back at her from the mirror looked tired. She rubbed the darkness under her eyes, hoping that the discoloration would disappear. She started to close her eyes to stop looking when she noticed new gray hairs at her temples. And despite all of what she was noticing was skin deep and could be addressed with rest, makeup, and a day at a spa, her desire and energy to make the effort was gone.

Callie kept her phone with her through her preparations to ensure that she did not miss Chase's call. As she walked toward her bed, she checked it again. The screen showed nothing had been either attempted or sent. She set the phone on her night table as she opened her Kindle to relax in someone else's story, somewhere else.

The vibration of her phone and sound of the Facetime ringtone pulled Callie back from her story. She fixed her hair to be presentable. She expected Chase would be several drinks into a stupor if he was using Facetime instead of the phone. After the fourth roll of the ringtone, Callie flipped the phone toward her to answer.

"Hi ,Mom!" Lizzie said with a smile as she framed the picture to her.

"Hi, sweetie," Callie replied while trying to hide her disappointment. "How are things at the beach?"

"OK," Lizzie said as she looked off to her left. "It's pretty cool here. I can see why everyone loves it so much. The water is so much warmer than Nantucket. And it's only May."

Callie smiled at Lizzie's comment. She hated the icy water in Nantucket but loved everything else about the island. The Outer Banks, particularly where Jason's cottage sat, was great from its oceanfront placement to the water temperature. She thought Jason's house, deck, and bench overlook were ideal. It needed more bedrooms and a larger common area, but its comfort, and the beach, were perfect.

"I knew you'd like it," Callie said as she continued to envision her time there. "You'll have to find that coffee shop I told you about. It's really cool and not too far from where Google Maps says you are."

Lizzie remained quiet after Callie recalled the coffee shop. She was not sure when the best time was to tell her that she had a job there and wanted to stay.

"I will, Mom," Lizzie lied.

"Just remember that the Outer Banks you're seeing now is not what it will be like after Memorial Day. Mr. Cart—" Callie paused to kill the mention of Jason's comments about the summer renters' impact on the businesses and traffic. She tried to think of another tack to take.

"I saw them," Lizzie interjected. "I saw Mr. Cartwright with Maya... In fact, it was at that coffee shop."

Lizzie saw Callie's face drop when she heard the news. She then regrouped to smile, realizing it was a good thing for her to know Maya, as well as Jason.

"That's certainly one of those small world things," Callie responded, wondering why God above would add that to her plate now.

"They were very nice. He was heading out of town. But Maya is living here for the summer to be a beach lifeguard."

Callie enjoyed the electricity in Lizzie's voice. She was happy with her trip to the beach and seeing Jason and Maya. Callie knew the beach trip would be a good transition between the end of classes and the start of summer. The Larson family trip to Nantucket was scheduled again in July instead of August. Lizzie was going to have four weeks of ocean time between her two trips.

"Is Maya living by herself this summer?"

"Yeah, she's staying at their beach house," Lizzie answered, "It's really coo... ol."

Lizzie regretted commenting about the cottage. She did not want to tell her mother she saw it or that she was snooping when Maya caught her. Although, in hindsight, it was funny. Mostly, she was afraid that her interest in the Cartwright family would hurt her mother after she severed all contact with Maya's dad.

Callie could see through her changes of expression that Lizzie had no intention of telling her that she saw Jason's cottage. She then wondered why she would share seeing him. Lizzie knew the history and situation.

"Maya's pretty cool," Callie said while recalling their first private conversation that brought them together. "I think you'd like her."

"Mom, I visited the cottage. We got a chance to talk," Lizzie confessed to further open the topic she let slip. "Oh, I also met a woman named Rebecca? She said to say hello and that she expected to see you this summer."

Callie smiled as she recalled her good, and tense, moments with Jason's friend and protector. Maya must have introduced Lizzie as her daughter.

"I think that's a long shot, sweetie," Callie answered. "Maybe. We still have Nantucket."

Lizzie could see Callie's expression fade with her comment. Nantucket was two months away, and her husband left her without saying goodbye. Lizzie waited for her mom to look before forcing a smile. Nantucket was also a vacation she was also dreading.

"Are you mad I saw them?" Lizzie asked.

"No. Why would I be?"

"Are you mad I went to their cottage?"

Callie paused to think about the question. As a practical matter, she was happy Lizzie met Maya and was comfortable with Jason. They were good people. Callie always thought Lizzie and Maya could be friends. The only bother for her was emotional. Her daughter had the opportunity she wanted to be involved with

Jason and his family. Callie was feeling jealous of the opportunity she also had and pushed away ten months earlier.

"Mom," Lizzie asked while pausing to build the courage to ask. "Can I stay here for the summer?"

Callie felt her soul pull from her body with the question. She was afraid of having to live with Chase after the wedding weekend reopened issues that seemed to have been put to bed. With Will in New York City, Lizzie would have been their buffer to make him behave.

"Oh, sweetie," Callie answered. "I don't think that's a good idea for this summer. You—"

"I have a place to live for free because Melissa's parents want her to have other people in the house when they're not here during the week."

"What about a job? You can't be a beach bum all summer."

Callie thought that working would push Lizzie to return home. Her job at the local coffee shop in Great Falls only lasted a few months before socializing with friends made working undesirable.

"I have a job," Lizzie finally admitted. "That's how I saw Mr. Cartwright and Maya. I work at that coffee shop you liked. The owner is friends with Mr. Cartwright."

Of course she is, Callie thought as she tried to find other objections to her staying.

"Lizzie, I just don't feel comfortable with you being there and relying on a family I don't know," Callie stated, hoping it was enough to convince her not to stay. "What happens if you need help?"

"Mr. Cartwright gave me a card with all his contact information on it. He took my cell number so I could call him. He said he'd pick up since he'd know the caller was me. He was really nice. He even endorsed me to Marie, who owns the coffee shop."

"A regular white knight," Callie mumbled as a frustrated smile appeared on her face.

"What?"

"Nothing, sweetie."

Callie's opposition to Lizzie started to shift as she thought about her living somewhere other than in the Northern Virginia craziness and on Nantucket with her parents struggling for two weeks. Lizzie's approach to asking, combined with her maturity through Callie's initial decline, was confidence building. Of course, Jason was again in her life, affecting it in a painful, but positive, way.

"Can I stay?" Lizzie asked again.

Callie looked at her baby's twenty-year-old face, excited to have an opportunity to live her life. She knew that either she could be there, or Lizzie could be home in six hours if needed. Visiting her over the summer would give Callie an opportunity to see Jason again without Chase around. She could get used to Clara, if she had to. If Lizzie came home, she knew she would be unhappy and make everyone else miserable in the process.

"Let's do this," Callie finally answered. "Why don't you use the two weeks you have to test if you really want to stay. If that works, you can stay if your dad agrees."

Lizzie stood and began hopping with excitement after hearing Callie's decision and conditions. She already knew she loved her coffee shop job, particularly after Jason got Marie to ease up with his endorsement. The house she was visiting was adequate with a comfortable bed and Wi-Fi. She was also excited to continue to see Maya and to spend time with her and her sisters at their oceanfront house. She knew her dad would not care either way. Her summer at the Outer Banks had just been blessed.

"Thanks, Mom, I'm so happy," Lizzie said. "I've got to go tell everyone. Love you! Bye!"

Lizzie disconnected the call before Callie could reply. Her excitement lifted Callie's spirits until her fast goodbye dropped them again. Callie needed to say *I love you too* back to her.

Realizing she just emptied her big house down to its last person, Callie sat to contemplate what it all meant. She remembered one of her first conversations with Jason about his divorce. He said the loneliness was the worst part. He also said it got better as time passed and the kids came around. His life now with Clara showed how the darkest moments work back to daylight and sunshine at some point. Like him twenty-eight years ago, when he regretted letting Callie go to find her ONE, Callie was feeling the same regret that she let him go find his ten months ago.

I heard you saw Lizzie at OBX

Callie keyed the text into her iPhone, then deleted it. She rewrote it again, holding her finger over the blue arrow that sends it. She knew that to push *Send* would open a variety of issues with and between her, Jason, Chase, and Clara. Callie closed her eyes to ask God for help. As she exhaled the anxiety that came with the decision, she touched the *Send* arrow.

# # #

Jason's eyes were closed as he dozed in an armchair. His iPhone, which his hands dropped on his chest when he fell asleep, gave a quick vibration and ping that woke him. Clara, who was next to him on the love seat, smiled as he jerked to the stimulus that was likely one of his kids wanting something. Jason's fog dissipated when he opened the text and sat up to look at the message. He keyed in a reply, hoping Callie was OK with his helping Lizzie.

Yes. A pleasant surprise. At our coffee shop.

"Who's texting you now?" Clara asked, noting a smile after he read the message.

"Callie," he answered honestly. "Maya and I ran into her daughter at the coffee shop before I left and she went to work. Her daughter, Lizzie, works there now."

Callie's name started Clara's brain. She was not jealous or angry that Callie was still texting her man. Her name brought to mind an image of her from the wedding weekend that grew larger to include other guests and her husband.

"OH.... MY.... GOD!" Clara shouted. "That's him!"

Jason watched as Clara transitioned from her normal quiet disposition to highly animated.

"Who?!" Jason replied in an excited voice. "Where?"

"BMW man," Clara said as she looked to the road leading back to the Flying Dutchman. "Pregnant Sarah's fiancé."

Jason stood to go see what Clara was looking at. He wanted to understand why she was so excited.

"I saw him when they drove in. He arrived late and went straight back to their cabin. I didn't see either of them at meal delivery." Clara stopped to recompile everything she saw, to be sure. "It has to be him."

"Who?"

"Callie's husband! What's his fucking name... CHASE!" Clara finally blurted out. "I think Chase is pregnant Sarah's fiancé!"

"No way," Jason replied, thinking through the possibility.

"Text Callie and see," Clara answered.

"Sure," Jason replied as he picked up his phone and pretended to type. "Callie. Is your husband in Asheville at our cabins with his pregnant mistress? ... Send."

The action irritated Clara. He did not believe what she had put together.

"No. Ask her if everything is OK this weekend," Clara thought out loud. "That should tell you if he's there."

Jason hesitated to work Callie just to test Clara's theory on the identity of pregnant Sarah's fiancé. Particularly when they could just wait until the morning.

"Send it," Clara said with a stare that said she would do it if he declined.

> *She was very sweet. Said she wished she could stay*
> *the summer. How are things at home?*

Clara rolled her eyes at the message. She objected to his playful reference to their coffee shop.

"Why did you throw all of that extra stuff in there? She's not going to answer you."

"Just wait," Jason answered as they both watched his screen in silence.

> *Idk shitty? he is on campaign in South Carolina.*
> *Spartanburg, I think. Western side.*

"Holy shit," Jason mumbled as he stared at Callie's reply. "I guess we'll know for sure in the morning."

Jason ran his fingers through his hair as he thought about the hurt this was going to inflict on Callie. He began to plot how to find out the truth and whether he should confront Chase, if it was him.

"Jason!" Clara called from the front desk. "Come here."

Jason entered the front hall to see Clara seated at the desk looking at the laptop used for registration. Its blue glow lit her face as its flickering light showed she was moving from document to document or image to image.

"Here!" she declared as she spun the laptop toward him. "That motherfucker is here."

Jason looked at the frozen, close-circuit television image from the Flying Dutchman that was time marked twelve hours earlier. The equipment Jason bought recorded on motion detection around the cabins. He installed it as security for guests and to prevent break-ins. When empty, spotlights came on at night. During storms, the mountain top looked like a Christmas tree as white lights turned on then off at each of the twelve cabins.

Clara's swearing surprised him. Even at her maddest moments,

Jason had never heard her use the F-bomb, let alone M-F anyone.

"I don't know how to deal with this," Jason said as he pondered how insane everything was becoming. "I suppose we could have him killed."

"Get serious. Then what," Clara replied. "The kid growing in Sarah's womb has no father, no provider. Callie's children... in particular, HER DAUGHTER... has no father."

Clara's nature toward life and animals favored preservation. Roadkill on the highway would upset her. Her cavalier response to Jason's extreme suggestion, although joking, showed that Clara had no respect for Chase's life. Her concern was likely for Sarah and her unborn child.

"This is so fucked up," Jason mumbled. "Sandy thinks Chase has spent all of their money, to include her inheritance. How do you deal with that?"

"I think she needs to cut the cord from that bastard and grab whatever she can," Clara replied, still angry.

"Let's think about this," Jason said. "Until we have a plan, he can't see either you or me. You'll need to get one of the staff to run their brunch tomorrow."

Jason closed the laptop to eliminate the image from his sight. He pulled out his phone to text Callie a reply to close their conversation.

I hope things work out. Half full, always. Lizzie
can call Maya for anything. Rebecca is there too. I'll
be back there in two weeks. Good Night.

Clara turned off the last light in the reading room as she moved to head upstairs. Jason let Zoe out for a pee before he followed Clara to bed. His worry for Callie was going to limit his sleep. His anger that Chase's narcissism and greed caused so much pain was going to carry forward until Jason could finish him.

#

As the early morning sunlight began to light the front yard and lily pond, Jason sat rocking back and forth in his favorite chair. A fresh, hot mug of coffee steamed as he held it level through his back-and-forth motion.

As expected, Jason did not sleep well. He tossed and turned until reaching the point of frustration to get up and caffeinated. The night was still dark when he first sat in his chair. He still had no plan for how to handle the day ahead. Abandoning his bed with Clara was also to ensure she would continue to sleep.

For most of his time alone, he thought about Callie asleep in her bed. How innocent she looked curled up with her hands usually near her face. He could see her sleeping as a twenty-two-year-old in his bed in Washington, DC, when he lived there and she visited. He envisioned her again as a fifty-year-old asleep in his bed on the first night they reconnected over Columbus Day weekend. Although the two images had twenty-eight years between them, the simple, common thread was that she was a beautiful human being who deserved to be loved.

Jason carried tremendous guilt from his past actions that hurt her deeply. He knew Chase was toxic and had to be removed from her life. His torment now sat with her. She had no place to land now that he was with Clara.

"Stressing?" Clara asked as she walked through the door.

She was carrying two cups of coffee. One was for her. The other was to replace his empty.

"I hope I didn't wake you," he replied as she sat beside him.

Clara smiled at the worried look on his face.

"You can't save the world, Jason," she answered. "Things have to work themselves out. Callie will survive this."

Clara's words were meant to both comfort him and to protect her. Her anger with Chase was partially due to his behavior. But it also had to do with the potential it had to destroy her relationship with Jason. Callie preceded Clara on Jason's personal timeline. He fell in love with her when love was its purest. Clara's deepest fear was that Callie would call him, and he would leave.

"It's just so brutal," Jason mumbled. "And she's so innocent and loving."

Clara watched him digest his own words as he took a pull of fresh coffee from his new mug. His expression fell flat as he stared at the water lilies that sat still on the pond in front of him.

"What are you thinking?" she asked, looking to get a framework on how the day was going to explode.

Jason's personality was not to let things sit. But his tactics in both problem solving and opportunity grasping were always thought through to the smallest detail. The two potential fatal flaws in his approach hinged on his blind devotion to Callie and his less than three hours of sleep before critical mass was going to be achieved.

The morning light that filtered through the leaves was Jason's favorite aspect of the cabin. As an early riser, he would sit alone on the deck gazing into the cascading rays that flowed through the gaps and illuminated the greenery.

Chase did not sleep well. Keeping Sarah separate from Callie was easy, given the demands of her job that required her time in South Carolina and his in Washington. As the Senator's senior aide, she spent most of her time with constituents, raising money and listening to ensure his votes coordinated with their wishes. That element of politics took a lot of personal touches. Sarah had the poise and intelligence to massage the most difficult situations to work for her boss. And when poise and intelligence were not enough, her beauty and charm worked well too. Chase often thought she would be a brilliant addition to his business. She did too.

When Callie's mother unexpectedly passed away, Chase was given the opportunity to change course back toward additional riches that he knew he was leaving behind when Callie's mother was healthy. Callie's father left Callie's inheritance to both of them when their marriage was strong. Her father expected it to last a lifetime.

Chase had no reason to believe that Callie's mother, Carolyn, would not do the same thing. Or at least leave what had been established earlier when her will was created. Callie never told him that Carolyn changed her will to leave everything to only her daughters with additional funds to each grandchild's trust. The sons-in-laws were left nothing.

Sarah's announcement that she was pregnant changed Chase's playing field. He expected she would demand to get married faster before showing her baby bump. Although he was not opposed to it, it would be better to have her end this pregnancy to try again later. But, at thirty-nine, bad timing was not an argument he could make even if she would be open to the idea. Chase took a pull of coffee as he looked to the illuminated leaves for inspiration.

With Mother Nature giving him no answers, Chase checked his phone for messages from Callie or anyone else. He was looking for something to take his mind away from his worries. With the sun rising, he knew he had over an hour before Callie would wake. He needed to plan a conversation with her away from Sarah. He opened his text screen to send her a message.

Can we talk at 10AM? Clients will be at church. Full day otherwise.

"Hey, baby daddy," Sarah called out as she slid open the door. "You left me in bed alone. This is supposed to be our couple's weekend."

Chase opened his arm to pull Sarah close as she sat next to him. His smile told her he was pondering something troubling. Her splendid news did not seem to be big enough to take away all of his worries. Even if for just a few days.

"Everything OK?" she asked while studying his face. "Worried about the campaign?"

Chase knew Sarah was sensing his tenseness. He was a good sleeper who would sleep past nine o'clock in the morning on weekends they were together. Their early bedtime the night before, despite being delayed by a few rounds of affection, should have relieved his tensions with sleep and exhaustion.

"Yes," Chase answered to take advantage of Sarah's opened door. "I'm concerned about next week and the entire summer."

Sarah reached across Chase's belly to pull herself to him.

"You're the best in the business," she whispered in his ear. "It'll all execute like clockwork."

Sarah kissed his cheek, happy to see a smile reappear on his face.

"It will, won't it." He smiled, still focused on the trees.

"You are the king maker," she added before giving him another soft kiss on his neck.

As Chase reveled in Sarah's praise and affection, he pulled her onto his lap to kiss her. As she moved, he noticed she was only wearing his long-sleeve t-shirt. With a slight adjustment to his robe and boxer shorts, they joined together again in nature that was around them, out of sight of the security cameras.

19

There was no brunch order to be delivered to the Flying Dutchman. Clara was not surprised, given that they were out for the day on Saturday. Brunch orders were unusual, unless a guest was staying at the cabin in seclusion and not heading out for day trips.

Jason remained puzzled about how to act. He talked with Clara about calling Callie to tell her the news. She could advise him on how she wanted their discovery disclosed. Clara thought to drop everything on Callie over the phone, and while she was alone, could be catastrophic. She did not think Callie had the strength to handle it alone. She did agree with Jason that Patty could be used for support. But that would require telling Patty everything before it was disclosed to Callie. There was no simple way to protect Callie's feelings. Jason being the messenger added another layer of pain.

Clara kept the security close-circuit feed from the Flying Dutchman on the screen of her laptop. Jason paced as he thought the morning away. His path included walking by the laptop to check for activity and change from the cabin. The BMW and the Mustang were still parked in the two parking slots by the cabin. Chase and Sarah were still inside.

"What are you going to do if they leave for the day?" Clara asked. "They check out tomorrow. There is time to do this right."

"I don't know," Jason said as he leaned close to the screen while running his fingers through his hair. "I just want to kill him... I really do."

Clara saw the tenseness in his face and moved to stand behind him. She put her hands on his shoulders to squeeze relief into his shoulders. His neck muscles were noticeably tight. As she attempted to work on his shoulders, Jason reached to grab both her hands with his. He then turned around to face her.

"I could have prevented this," he said, struggling to deal with the looming outcome.

"How?" Clara answered. "How could you possibly have kept this from happening?"

Jason dropped his head as he held on to her hands. He knew he did everything right to convince Callie to find and want him again. He knew his advice to resolve her marriage issues free of him was right to ensure her head was in the right place for them to start again. What he did not see was a narcissist husband who either would not, or could not, let go of her while living a parallel life with another woman.

"Do you think Sarah knows he's still married?"

"Married!" Jason laughed out of frustration. "He's supposed to be getting back together with his wife. She was probably the affair he promised to get rid of when Carolyn was dying."

Jason shook his head as he turned back to the computer screen. Everything was the same as before. He decided to get a glass of juice and to help Clara in the kitchen. His hope was that by staying near Clara some divine inspiration may come his way.

After loading the last glass, Jason started the dishwasher to clean the containers from Saturday night's food deliveries. He grabbed a dish towel to dry his hands and wander back to the front desk to check the computer screen again.

The image of the Flying Dutchman was the same as it was when they started to clean the dishes. With the two cars in the parking slots, they were still in the cabin. The time stamp on the computer said fifteen minutes before ten o'clock. But to him, it felt like fifteen minutes to five in the afternoon. He knew he needed more caffeine. With a Monday check-out, Jason thought they were likely still in bed. And he wanted to deal with Chase today.

Jason returned to the kitchen to find the coffee maker empty and turned off. He thought for a moment on whether more coffee was the answer to his exhaustion. He checked the refrigerator for something cold that would deliver the same boost as coffee without having to either wait or work for it. Near the back sat a pitcher of sweet tea. Clara brewed it with a potent black tea that had a rich flavor and solid caffeine kick.

"Bingo," Jason said as he pulled the pitcher from the refrigerator.

"Jason!" Clara called from the front desk. "Chase is leaving the cabin."

Jason grabbed a glass as he carried the pitcher with him. As he walked into the front hall, Clara was seated in the chair, waiting. She had the same determination to nail Chase. But she wanted it to be when Sarah was not around.

"I feel like an idiot hiding on our own property," Clara mumbled as she studied the screen. "I want to nail this asshole."

"I hope he prepaid for the cabin," Jason asked while pouring his glass of tea.

"Nope," Clara answered. "She did."

Jason leaned in to the screen for a better look of what Chase was wearing. He knew he could stand at the end of the drive to the Dutchman for Chase to drive by when leaving. His concern with that plan was Chase actually running into him, then taking off.

A closer look showed Chase was wearing running shorts and shoes. He was wearing a James Madison University dry-wick shirt that Lizzie probably bought for him as a present. Jason's drawer was full of university swag from each of his daughters' schools. That Chase was wearing Lizzie's college shirt while hiding away with his mistress was heartless. Jason shared a look and brief laugh with Clara about Chase's attempt to exercise.

As Chase began his run, he took off up the driveway and out of view of the camera. Knowing the property, and having run it from the Dutchman many times, Jason expected Chase to stay on the property by running to, then up, the main drive to the top of the mountain where the three empty lots sat.

Chase arrived at the bottom of his cabin's driveway and made the expected turn to take him up the hill. Jason and Clara watched through the window as Chase ran by. Both noticed he was struggling. They knew that at some point, the climb of the hill would get him.

As Chase disappeared into the trees, Jason slipped out the front door to run around the pond. His run to reach the top of the mountain was shorter from the street-side meadow instead of the winding road back that accessed a number of the farm's cabins on the hillside.

Clara did not hear Jason slip away. When Zoe followed and banged through the front door, she realized he was gone. By the time Clara reached the door to see what his plan was, Zoe had caught him as he was finishing his run around the pound and about to head into the trees. Clara grabbed the key fob to the Volvo that was parked next to the main house. She knew that Jason would not do anything to physically harm Chase. She just wanted to be there to stop him if she was wrong.

# # #

The stone bridge normally used to cross the creek was covered but visible. The recent rain raised the creek level that submerged the stones and a dry crossing. The path from the creek led to the hillside meadow Jason showed Callie on her first night at the farm. Zoe followed by plowing through the water as she always did when out with Jason.

The run up the hill was easier than the road. Its pitch was steeper, but the length was much shorter. When Jason reached the top plateau, he ran past the mountain lots and began to work his way back down the fire road that led to the drive Chase was climbing. As he made his way farther than he expected, he began to slow his descent. He wanted Chase's exposure to be a wicked surprise and to have a crippling impact. He stopped to wait on the upper end of a blind corner on the road.

Clara was uncertain what to expect when she reached either Chase or the two men together. Her concern was that Chase would be desperate enough to finish Jason if he got the upper hand in a scuffle. She returned to the main house for the shotgun Tom bought for protection. The box of shells was in the drawer at the base of the cabinet that stored the weapon. Clara put the shells in her pocket as she carried the twelve-gauge to the Volvo.

The road stayed silent while Jason and Zoe waited for Chase to arrive. Jason expected Chase's overweight, out-of-shape physique would struggle on the hill climb. Jason was fully rested from his run to deal with any attack Chase might consider trying. Deep down, he was hoping Chase was that desperate. But he also knew, just as it was during their beach scuffle, he could not hurt him. Callie would not forgive him for giving Chase a beating.

Clara drove slowly up the main drive hill with the windows down to listen for any signs that the two men had found each other. The winding road was bordered by dense vegetation that was perfect for afternoon walks out of the sun and heat. It also created too many blind spots around corners. Driving too quickly had the potential to put her on top of things before she would see or be able to stop for it.

# # #

Callie woke at her usual 8 a.m. The sun was shining through her unshaded window. On an ordinary day, she would sit up, refreshed and ready with a list of things to accomplish. But when she woke to confirm the time, her body felt tired. Her desire to move ahead for the day was zapped. She fell back into a light sleep as she grabbed and curled next to her body pillow.

At 10 a.m., Callie woke to a vibration noise on her nightstand.

Her reach to pick up her phone was not long enough through the pillow she had between her and her phone. Concerned about missing the call, Callie pushed herself up to a sitting position that enabled her to grab her phone to answer. As her screen illuminated, she saw Chase's name and face staring back at her.

"Chase," she answered in a clear voice, now fully awake with her heart pounding.

"Good morning," Chase opened softly, hoping to set a friendly tone for the call.

Chase had settled onto a boulder by the side of the road two hundred yards up the road from the main house. The surrounding air was full of sounds as insects and birds chattered and screeched. The temperature was cool, giving him an immediate relaxation as he started another stressful call with his wife.

"I just wanted to check in," he said. "Let you know everything is going well."

Callie closed her eyes to his comments. His detachment was being proven through his narcissistic focus on her concern for him. Her thoughts, however, changed when she heard the loud sounds of nature behind him.

"Where are you?"

Chase looked around as he pulled together his lie.

"I'm in Spartanburg... at the hotel," he answered.

"Sounds like you're in the jungle."

Chase tensed at Callie's comment. The surrounding noise became louder after she mentioned it. The added sound of an engine and grinding gravel gave a more city backdrop to their call. He was near another driveway. He thought the nearby car was just another guest.

"I just—" Chase stopped when a familiar Volvo appeared from around the lower corner, then stopped.

"Just what?" Callie replied.

"I'll have to call you back."

The line went dead as Callie waited for her husband to finish the sentence he started. She looked at her phone to see if the line was still active. Her main screen appeared, saying the call had ended.

Callie considered calling him back. But his fast cut-off meant that something important was taking his attention away from his estranged wife and saving their marriage. She put the phone back on her nightstand and clutched her pillow in blank thought.

20

The celery-green Volvo Cross Country wagon was eerily familiar. Callie drove a silver one when their children were small. He felt a panic set in as he thought about the possibility of who the driver was. But the odds were better that it was someone else.

Clara was surprised to reach Chase before Jason. She drove slowly so that, at worst, they would converge on him at the same time. Seeing him sitting on the boulder made sense. He was heavy and out of shape. The run up the incline of the mountain road was a challenge for fit runners. As he stood to face the car, Clara stayed still with the engine running. She then shifted into park.

Chase could not see either the shape or face of the car's driver through the windshield. He waited for several seconds, after hearing the car shift into Park, for the driver to emerge. When he, or she, did not step out, he started to walk toward the car.

Clara grabbed the shotgun that was sitting in the seat next to her as Chase started to move toward her. She knew it was not loaded. To ready it would require getting out to remove the shells from her pocket before attempting to load a gun she had not fired in years. As Chase grew closer, he felt relief to make out the smaller, female shape of the driver. His thoughts of facing off with Jason started to recede.

Clara felt stuck in her position. Chase had slowed his approach, weaving and squinting to look in the car from a distance. With nowhere to turn around, and only Chase to drive through, Clara's only option was to drive by him, exposing her and Jason in the process. To remain still would attract him to the car. Clara decided to step out with the empty gun handy to scare him back, if needed.

Chase stopped his approach when he heard the click of the latch and saw the driver door start to open. The face of the woman getting out was shielded by the door as she bent to bring something with her. That all changed when Clara showed her face while keeping the shotgun hidden behind the door.

"Just stop where you are," Clara said nervously.

Chase's face clenched to a frustrated smile as he recognized the woman he met a week earlier in Great Falls. He noticed that she looked prettier than he remembered. Her hair pulled back and the less formal look worked better than how she looked all dressed up at the reception.

"Now I know why you were able to fall and catch those flowers," Chase said, trying to charm his way through.

He started to walk toward the car as he spoke. As he took his steps, Clara exposed the shotgun.

"Jason's coming down from the top of the mountain with his dog."

Chase smiled at what seemed like an idle threat. Jason would have either driven up with her, or by himself, if he was there.

"Sure he is," Chase said as he took another step to test her resolve. "Why are you here chasing after me? In fact, why are you here, up in the fucking mountains of North Carolina?"

"Because she's with me. And you're on my property," replied a male voice from behind.

Chase turned to see Jason approaching at a walking pace. He stepped up his gait when he heard Clara's voice address Chase, to ensure Chase could not reach her if he thought they were alone. When he saw her through the trees with a shotgun in her hands, he slowed to not startle the situation. Clara had the ability to defend herself.

"What is it with you?" Chase remarked as Jason slowed to a stop. "I just can't fucking get you out of my life."

Jason remained still as Zoe sniffed the foliage off to the side. His calm kept her off alert that any imminent danger was in the area for her number one.

"What life is that?" Jason replied as he moved his eyes from Chase to Clara, then back. "Narcissistic? Cheating? Baby daddying? What?"

"Why do you even care, man?" Chase answered. "You've got your beautiful woman right there! With a freaking shotgun. Let my wife go, for God's sake."

Zoe redirected her attention to Jason as he tensed and took a step toward Chase. She reoriented to his side, waiting for her master to say something. Clara's eyes met Jason's as she waited for him to act.

"Not until you do," Jason answered calmly while taking another step closer.

Chase tensed further as he watched Jason approach with his dog while having his girlfriend behind him with a shotgun.

"This isn't a fair fight," Chase remarked while looking at the three prongs of Jason's attack.

"I should beat you for the pain you've caused," Jason answered.

Chase laughed at the comment. He was looking at the man who splattered his fiancée just before their wedding. Chase was Callie's white knight to pick up those pieces.

"Put your dog in the car, and tell your honey to stay out of it, and I'll go," Chase answered, "What do I have to lose now? Actually, it might feel good."

Chase squared to face Jason, ready to take his assault. Clara grew concerned as she watched Jason counter with a step to improve his balance while opening and closing his hands. She knew Zoe would be on Chase as soon as the men came together. She was also concerned about injury to her and Jason if Zoe grabbed the wrong limb.

The sound of the blast crippled the intentions of both men as it shocked them to a bent position and echoed through the valley.

"NO!" Clara yelled to intervene on the senseless pounding that was about to happen. "This ends right now."

Jason and Chase both stood as Clara moved from the car. The shotgun was still smoking from the single blast. Both men knew she had one more shell loaded to discharge.

"I'm going to solve this," Clara commanded as she pointed the barrel at Chase. "You! Are going to come clean with both your wife and your baby momma. I'm sure you're lying to both of them. You have until the end of the day. And then you're to get the fuck off our property. Sarah can stay. Or she can leave with you. No refund either." Clara smiled as she looked to Jason for approval. "Know I have both of their contact information," Clara added. "And I'm going to call them both in the morning to check on them, ask if they've talked to you, then tell them what I know. After that, I couldn't care less if they're stupid enough to take you back."

Chase remained silent as Clara gave her orders. His anger was gone as fear entered his mind and body with what he had to do. Sarah would definitely leave him and get him fired from the campaign. He had been lying to her about Callie and their divorce. Waiting on the estate money would not be a good enough answer for his lies. Callie would, without hesitation, divorce him once she knew about his continued affair and the child he had fathered.

Jason watched Chase deflate. He felt relief that Callie's torment would soon be over. He had seen a renewed light in her eyes when she visited ten months earlier after deciding to divorce him the first time. He felt no joy in knowing he was right to tell her to not let him back into her life. But it was necessary for Callie to learn that on her own as their final separation process.

"OK," Chase surrendered. "I'll do it."

"Today! Now go!" Clara ordered without conferring with Jason.

As Chase walked back down the hill past the Volvo, he kept his eyes forward and down. Clara looked to Jason to see how he was handling the resolution she dictated without getting the satisfaction of either giving input or beating Chase. She saw that he was smiling and shaking his head in disbelief. As Chase fell from view, he walked to her, still holding a smile full of pride.

"Remind me never to get you really angry at me."

Clara set the gun next to the car. Although high on adrenaline, her demeanor showed that something was troubling her.

"Someone had to be the cool head," she answered softly as she hugged him.

Chase was now exposed to ending his ride with Callie. And it was going to be painful. What was happening to him was exactly the position Chase enjoyed doing to his clients' opponents when disclosures of damaging information suddenly appeared at just the right time.

Jason knew Chase's pain was going to be worse and last longer than the beating he wanted to give him. He was happy to have created a path to freedom for Callie.

"I love you," Jason whispered, as he continued to hold Clara tightly.

"I know," she replied as she squeezed him tightly. "You don't have to whisper."

Although Jason either did not see it or was afraid to admit it, Clara's intuition was sensing a pull that was separating him from her that she, and he, had to address in their own way.

The two-week Cartwright-girl July reunion with Dad started

as scheduled. Jason arrived early to prepare the cottage and to enjoy the time alone with his kids. Clara stayed behind to manage the cabins that were rented to capacity through Labor Day. Each afternoon ended with Rachel's special margaritas, then morphed into the legendary Abbie happy hours as all the owners came together to celebrate the rites of summer. Rebecca was glad to have her friend back at the beach.

Jason continued to talk to Callie to ensure she was doing well and that Chase had made the full confession he promised on the mountain. They agreed she needed time to process it all and to execute the divorce. Jason offered his cottage to her, as well as any available cabin, as a getaway to start the healing process. Their conversations never directed back to them as a couple. It was a topic Jason did not want to discuss with her. It was a convenient crutch Callie knew she could not lean on, even if offered.

Jason started to lean on Callie's sister, Patty, as an ongoing source to ensure Callie was in a good place and improving. His relationship with Callie's older sister rebounded after Callie's first visit in October. His behavior and advice during that time, to include stopping a possible mistake of infidelity for her youngest sister, healed their old wounds to become friends. Jason extended the same invitation to Patty if she, Brian, and her boys ever wanted to visit the beach or were in the Asheville area.

"Mind if I sit with you?" a familiar voice asked from behind.

Jason was seated on the deck overlooking the beach. He was enjoying the satisfaction of seeing his girls sun near the waterline along with Lizzie and her housemate. His eyes would roll over them as he watched others play and swim in the water. His habit to stand when a woman entered the room was automatic, even if from behind, on his deck, overlooking the water.

"I'm so glad to see you." He smiled as he hugged her.

The feel of her body and smell of her perfume rejuvenated his senses. He offered her a seat and any refreshment she wanted from his assortment of cold drinks in his cooler.

"This is awesome," she said as she looked up and down the coastline.

"It is," he answered.

Jason watched her survey the surroundings she already knew. She smiled when she looked to find him watching her.

"I thought I'd stop by to visit before heading down to see Lizzie," she explained, following her words with a slight smile. "But I see she's here."

"Yup," Jason replied. "She's part of the family now, comfortable to grab what she wants, when she wants it."

Callie laughed at the comment, remembering his same reply when she did not bring him a coffee on her first morning at the cottage over Columbus Day weekend. As that image faded in her head, her expression went blank with it.

"I'm sorry I haven't called," Callie started. "I really appreciated how you handled things when you confronted Chase, and that you let me deal with all of it."

Jason's eyes closed as he smiled.

"You can thank Clara for that." He chuckled. "I, personally, wanted to kick the shit out of him."

As he reopened his eyes, he found Callie gazing at him. Her head was nodding in agreement as she seemed to be visualizing what could have happened.

"Then thank her too," she answered. "And for not shooting him. I'm hitting him hard for alimony."

Callie gave Jason a slight push to show she was joking and to bring him fully into their conversation. She saw in his face that he was still struggling.

"He got fired from that South Carolina campaign. Seems like his business was in a spiral I didn't hear about. I don't know what's going on with his baby-mama. As much as that should hurt me, I'm really sad for her, and that child."

Callie shook her head as she thought about Chase's implosion.

"Why do you think you and I not only circled back to something that crashed and burned so badly when we were kids, but so desperately held on to hope that it could happen for us now?" he asked to bring her back.

"Because it was so right back then, and so easy and natural now."

Jason took a deep breath, then exhaled. The woman who had captivated him for decades was next to him, and available. There was an undeniable love that pulled both ways. He reached to push some hair that had fallen by her temple back behind her ear. Her tan face and chestnut-brown hair melted his heart.

Callie smiled as her eyes returned to the waterline to see Lizzie emerge from the surf. Lizzie's excitement to see her mom sitting on the bench above the dune showed in her smile and wave. Callie was delighted to see her youngest happy during a time that could be complete darkness for a child. She glanced at Jason, then back as she waved back.

"This has saved her," Callie remarked as she turned to him. "And... YOU saved me."

"It gets better, I promise."

Callie nodded her head in agreement as she watched Lizzie frolic in the water with Maya. The old Callie would have cried while finalizing the separation both knew was happening. But her new strength enabled her to stay strong. Just like her anger did when dealing with Chase and his lawyers.

"Anything new with you?" Callie asked to redirect the conversation away from her sadness.

Jason studied Callie's face for signs that her head and heart were in a position to handle what he needed to tell her. Her resolute statements about Chase, his demise, and her compassion for the woman and child that helped take him from her said she was in a good space to talk candidly.

"Give me a minute," Jason said as he stood.

Callie gave a puzzled look as he turned to walk back to the cottage. As he disappeared from sight, Callie turned to watch Zoe and Molly nag the girls to throw Zoe's floating fake duck. It was a training tool that Jason bought to fling into the surf to occupy and exercise Zoe on walks. Callie squinted to see what the object was, then felt sad when she realized it was a fake, dead, rubber duck.

"OK," Jason said nervously as he sat back down next to her.

Callie noticed a dramatic shift in his demeanor as he settled in. She turned to look at him as he thought about how to say what he wanted to tell her.

"Clara and I had a long talk after we sent Chase packing from the farm," Jason started. "In fact, it was Clara that moved this to the forefront. I think I was just settled into contentment that she and I would just cruise through the rest of our lives."

Callie began to sense what Jason was starting to tell her. It was obvious he was struggling inside with his feelings and thoughts. Callie could feel her jaws clenching as her lip began to quiver.

Jason leaned into the bench as he reached to pull a small box from his pocket. Callie knew from its shape what it contained. Her eyes began to well up as he opened it to show her an engagement ring.

"That looks like the ring I gave back to you thirty years ago," she said, surprised that a ring he would buy for Clara would be so similar.

"Twenty-eight years ago," he corrected as he smiled. "And it IS the ring you gave back to me twenty… eight… years ago."

Callie was confused why he still had the ring and why he was showing it to her now.

"I could never let it go. I brought it with me when I first moved here. And I want you to have it."

Callie accepted the box as she studied the ring that was inside it. Its size was bigger than she remembered.

"I remember the jeweler commenting, small hand, big rock, when I bought this," Jason joked. "And that was before I added the baguettes."

Callie smiled as she shifted her attention from the ring in the box back to Jason.

"What's this all about?"

Jason shuffled as he settled to explain his reason for giving her the ring now.

"I love Clara Haigh," he started. "She's wonderful and we have a lot in common and have a lot of fun together. But she said to me that she and I don't have what you and I have. What she and her dead husband, Tom, had. And she said it was unfair for her to not let me explore that."

"Sounds a lot like what you told me when I took your bait to show up here," Callie said, anxious to hear what else he had to say.

Jason smiled at her remark. He agreed that taking the practical approach to researching options could bring the right answer. But his history with Callie showed him that taking time to figure things out could eliminate the best choice simply because the timing did not work out for the other person. Clara knew if Tom ever reappeared that she would choose him over Jason. She had to give Jason the same opportunity to live his optimum life too. She knew, regardless of how things ended, that Jason would let her stay to run Fox Farm for as long as she wanted.

"I told her I didn't want to risk losing her when things with you, and between you and me, are, and have been, so dicey."

Jason saw Callie's face drop with his comment. Her mind shot back through images of them breaking apart in the past as young lovers, then later over the past two years.

"But I just can't ignore how I feel about you." he continued. "The need to know where you are… how you are doing… and to feel you next to me is so intense that I cannot let you go. And Clara knows that. She could feel it in the air. She could see it in my face every time you were near or when your name was mentioned."

Callie looked back at the ring. Her heart was pounding as she resisted the urge to jump into his arms.

"Jason," she said, starting to cry. "What are you saying? I don't want to come between you and Clara if that's what you want. I'm not a pity case for you to save."

A tear dropped from Jason's eye as he smiled back at her.

"You, Mary Calista… young Callie, are the love of my life. My ONE. I'm giving this ring back to you because I never should have taken it back from you. I'm not asking you to marry me. I'm asking you to love me again like you did back then. And to share your life and love with me for the rest of our lives."

Callie wiped her tears as she leaned toward him.

"Are you asking me to live with you, in sin?" she asked, laughing through her words.

"Until death do us part," he answered as she jumped into his arms.

As Jason stood, lifting Callie with him, neither of them noticed their collective five daughters, and friend, watching from the shoreline. Maya smiled as she watched what she thought was best for her dad, happen.

"You guys owe us twenty bucks each," she said to Elyse and Rachel. "The ten Faith and I paid you, and the ten you owe us from the Clara/Callie bet."

ABOUT THE AUTHOR

Milo Hays

Milo Hays has spent his career bookending entrepreneurial business development with fundraising counsel services to non-profits. All the ventures involved convey-ing visions and stories in a story-telling manner to excite emotions to either invest, buy or donate. Milo Hays novels focus on mid-life characters working through life change events when existing life paths come to forks in the road.

BOOKS BY THIS AUTHOR

Two Once Removed Collection

Two Once Removed
Two Once There
Two Once Settled

1200 Miles

When Jamie Stewart travels from San Diego to Portland, Oregon to buy his childhood dream car to drive back down the California coast, the seller's elderly widow asks to travel with him on the trip she always wanted to take in the car.

Jamie's time and experience with her with the addition of his eldest daughter adds the life color of three generations with different perspectives sharing a ride, solving life's problems and ultimately identifying what is most important in life.

Dervish Red

It all starts when the obviously lost, distinguished looking, fish-out-of-water first walked into her hopping, backwoods country winery bar, she just could not help but tease him, and find him wickedly attractive.

Rowan Delaney, a burned out, fifty-year-old, soon-to-be-divorced, banker needed to relieve some stress. When he takes a day-drive out into the countryside one Saturday, he finds himself out in the middle of nowhere desperately needing to pee. The only place his phone GPS could find with a suitable, public rest room, is a small, country winery and bar tucked back into the trees. What was to be a quick pit stop introduces him to the winery's feisty, beautiful, fifty-year-old owner who quickly locks onto him to make him feel uncomfortable while also, surprisingly, grabs his heart.

Can a true love story survive, when city and country cultures clash over wine?

Funny, heartwarming, and enlightening, Dervish Red is a story about rebirth in life, love, and career at a truly unusual place.

Made in United States
North Haven, CT
15 April 2022

18291847R00108